The Connection

more than expected

Vida Brown

Table of Contents

Prologue

The evening air is cool and moist, saturated from a recent rain shower, and a misting of dew covers the trees. A small family is gathered in the clearing, two parents and a young girl; they marvel at the blue and emerald green foliage arcing over their heads and forming a sparse canopy in the sky.

The girl, about three years old, sits on the cold, dark grass and traces her fingers through its wet blades. There are tiny, phosphorescent dots sprinkled across the ground, seemingly buried just beneath the dirt. She sits up and pushes herself forward; the lights seem to beckon to her with a silent call.

Her parents stand behind her, speaking in hushed voices. She slides her fingers further down, pushing aside the dense clumps of grass to get to these strange bulbs of light. Every time she nearly grabs one, it shimmies away slightly and just barely escapes her grasp. She lets out a small, high-pitched noise of frustration.

There is a small pond in the center of the clearing, reflecting the moonlight from above. The girl's mother steps towards the pond and leans over its edge to peer into it. The water is dark and churning, dotted with small balls of light just like the ones in the grass. When she looks up at the sky, no stars are in sight. Only the full moon, just peaking at its highest point and perfectly centered between the branches of the trees that arch around it.

The girl's father joins her mother at the edge of the pond, and they exchange serious glances.

"What kind of sign is this?" he asks her, looking down at the disturbed water. "I've never seen it so dark."

She closes her eyes and breathes in deeply, taking in the cold air around her and letting it fill her lungs with its crisp determination.

"Something is waiting for her," she murmurs before opening her eyes and looking back at him. They both turn around to look at their child, still struggling on her knees in the grass to catch one of the tiny creatures. "I don't know what, but... we need to protect her."

She looks at the man beside her, her brow creased with worry. He reaches out and grabs her hand to squeeze it tightly.

"We might have to leave," she continues, voice cracking over the last word. "Do you understand what I'm saying right now? We might..." She trails off and takes another deep breath, this one shakier than the last.

"I know," he soothes, rubbing his thumb across her wrist. "I understand. We'll be okay. *She* will be okay."

"How can you be sure?" she asks. "I'm not even sure."

"You'll protect her; I trust you." He gives her a small smile, hiding his worry. She sees right through him and smiles back before leaning forward to press a delicate kiss against his cheek.

Suddenly, the girl who was so focused on picking up one of the lights fluttering around in the grass leans back and sits on her feet. She closes her eyes.

Her parents, still standing by the pond, feel the wind pick up around them suddenly. The air grows even chillier in half a second, and goosebumps rise along the skin on their arms. They instinctively bundle together and turn towards the girl.

The wind picks up more and more, dragging leaves and dead pieces of grass from the ground to whirl about the clearing in an invisible cyclone. The water begins to churn faster, moving aggressively and sloshing onto the dirt around its edges.

The girl's parents start to move towards her, but a gust of wind pushes them back, nearly toppling them over into the water. The mother clutches tightly onto the father as his foot slips behind him and he buckles backward.

She pulls him forward just enough to keep him on dry land, and they manage to step away from the pond.

Their daughter doesn't lose focus for a second; her eyes remain closed the whole time.

All the wind seems to circle her, dubbing her as its center and whipping the grass around her in a wild dance. The lights that had buried themselves beneath the surface begin to rise.

They float up in the air all around her, every last one, and light up the clearing like a thousand fiery lanterns. Her parents gaze around them with wide eyes as the wind finally settles and these small orbs of light dance and sway before their eyes.

The lights that were skimming across the water float upward, too, and join the rest. Finally, the young girl opens her eyes.

A wide grin spreads across her youthful face and she stands on wobbly legs. She reaches out to touch one of the lights, but they bob and weave just out of her grip. She lets out a string of high-pitched giggles and runs in a circle, still shooting her arms out above her to try and capture just one.

Her mother slowly approaches her and lets out a relieved gush of air. She watches as her daughter prances around the clearing and folds her arms together. "She might be even more than we bargained for," she says, turning to look at her mate. He raises his eyebrows and nods.

"That's one way to put it," he kids, turning back to watch their daughter. He walks up to her and takes one of her hands in his before adding, "I think we all have a long road ahead of us."

Chapter 1

The seed is sown

"Gisela… *Gisela*!"

The sharp click of stiletto heels reverberates through the hallway as Gisela's manager, Katherine, speeds from her office toward Gisela's cubicle.

Gisela rolls her eyes, groans, and slams her face into her hands. *Where else does she expect to find me besides here?* she thinks to herself. Her best friend, Sophia, rolls her chair back from her own small space and peeks over at Gisela.

"Look out!" she hisses playfully. "The witch is approaching."

Gisela shoots her a mocking scowl but shoots up straight as soon as Katherine walks through the doorway. Sophia pulls herself back to her desk at lightning speed and the two women manage to pretend, with poise, they were simply working moments before.

Katherine glances between them with narrowed eyes before loudly clearing her throat.

Gisela slowly turns around and looks at her boss before raising an eyebrow. "You were calling for me?" she asks, barely containing the irritation from her voice.

"Yes, I was, as a matter of fact," Katherine snaps. "Didn't you hear me? I think the whole office did."

"Oh, I did hear you," Gisela responds. "But it sounded like you were on your way here anyway. And this *is* my cubicle, after all, so I don't know why you thought you needed to go on a missing person's hunt for me."

"Listen, Ms. Schäfer," Katherine continues, a scowl quickly filling up her face, "I'm at my wits end with you already today, so I do *not* want to hear any more of your characteristic snottiness."

"Yes, ma'am," Gisela replies with a nod. She cocks her head, honey-colored hair she's half-pulled back with a claw clip draping gracefully over her shoulder. She crosses one leg over the other and folds her hands in her lap. "I'm listening."

Katherine stammers for a second before shaking her head and crossing her arms. Her blonde hair, styled in perfect curls, is pulled back in the same style. She absentmindedly touches the clip and frowns ever so slightly.

Gisela looks over at Sophia, who is convenietnh absorbed by whatever document is pulled up on her computer screen and is holding a hand to her mouth. However, Gisela can just barely make out the corner of her lips twisted upward in a smile. She smiles to herself, knowing full well her friend is currently holding back laughter.

"Gisela, over here," Katherine says with a finger snap. She smooths her hands over her pencil skirt and takes in a short, deep breath with an abrupt exhale right after.

Gisela looks back up at her and focuses her full attention. *Okay, I've delayed her tongue lashing long enough,* she thinks ruefully. *Let's see what she can nitpick me for today.*

"What was the deal with that paperwork you filed yesterday for your client's new hires?" Katherine asks.

She can't even hide the smirk on her face? Gisela wonders.

"What part of the paperwork are you referring to, exactly?" she asks.

"The part where you wrote the date incorrectly on not one, but *two* of the files for their new hires. Thankfully, I had a feeling I should look over your work this time and managed to catch it before sending it off to the company. Are you sure you can keep up with this company's pace? You know, attention to detail is extremely important here."

By the time Katherine finishes, she has a faint expression of satisfaction on her face. She discreetly looks Gisela up and down. "Maybe this workplace just isn't well suited for someone with your… unique disposition."

Gisela feels her face flush but with anger rather than embarrassment. *Doesn't she have anything better to do than harass me all the time?*

"You know, I did fill out about fifty of those sheets yesterday, as I'm sure you realize. I'm very sorry I miswrote the date on two of them, but as far as I'm aware, that doesn't really affect their business after all. The date merely denotes which day I logged the event of an employee's hiring."

She takes a deep breath after her reply and starts tapping her foot against her leg. "Also," she continues, "I'm not sure what you are referring to by my 'unique disposition,' but I can assure you it has held me back in no way during my time here. In fact, the regional manager has made it very clear to me that my productivity has been consistently high."

Katherine's face darkens and immediately shifts into a blank stare. "You're really testing my last nerves," she huffs. Her voice is high-pitched and the vein on her neck is visibly strained. "Just because the date on the paperwork wouldn't have consequences in this instance doesn't mean it doesn't reflect on your overall capabilities. How do I know you won't start making bigger mistakes on your paperwork? You're toeing the line, Ms. Schafer, so I suggest you be on guard." She takes a step back towards the door before pausing. Her eyes move down to Gisela's shoes and she lets out a short, airy laugh.

"Oh, dear, don't tell me those are *knockoff* Prada loafers? I know how obsessed you are with convincing everyone you come from money, but come on now."

Gisela frowns and meets Katherine's gaze; their blue eyes seem to flash at each other in a silent struggle. Now Sophia is half turned around in her seat, watching them with wide eyes.

In a flash, Gisela whips off one black loafer to expose her stockinged foot and holds it out towards Katherine.

"Take another look, ma'am," she replies with a curt voice. "See the metal logo on the last shoelace hole?" She turns it so that Katherine can see the inside. "And the red stripe on the sole? You can even feel the leather and the stitching if you'd like."

Katherine's face flares up like a tomato before she folds her arms. "No, thank you," she practically snarls.

Gisela shrugs and slips her foot back into the shoe.

Katherine whirls around and starts to leave, but Gisela makes a tutting sound to get her attention. She stops in the doorway, refusing to look back.

"For the record, Ms. Katherine, I don't need to convince anyone I come from money because I do. Anytime you ask, I'd love to introduce you to my Oma."

Katherine sucks her teeth and rolls her eyes before leaving, fists clenched at her side and heels clacking just as loudly as they did when she arrived.

As soon as they can't hear her anymore, Sophia propels her chair several feet back from her desk, wheels scraping against the carpet, and gapes openly at Gisela.

"*Oh. My. Gosh*," she hisses, shaking her head in bewilderment. "You just totally laid the smackdown on Ms. Katherine."

"What do you mean?" Gisela asks. She flashes an incredulous smile. "I just told her the truth, like I always do."

"Girl, I love you," Sophia declares before erupting in a fit of giggles.

Gisela's smile slowly stretches into a grin before she can't help but join in the laughter, and soon the two of them are pushing and pulling each other's chairs and swatting each other playfully on the arm.

Sometime between laughing and gasping for air, Gisela asks, "Hey, have you ever thought about leaving? Me and you, quitting, starting our own business or something?"

"What?" Sophia asks with a loud bark of laughter. "Girl, you crack me up. She tucks a dark, stray curl behind her ear.

Gisela sighs and rests her chin in her hand. "A girl can dream."

***

As Gisela winds down and tunes back into her work, she has a hard time dismissing the thought of leaving from her head. She glances over at Sophia from time to time, but her friend is fully wrapped up in virtual consultations.

Maybe I should try to practice what Oma Bast wants me to, she thinks as she absentmindedly watches Sophia from the corner of her eye. She's thankful her friend gets so hyper-focused because she thinks she is being pretty obvious about leaning back and observing her.

Gisela's Oma has raised her to become more and more in tune with the spiritual and psychic energy all around them; she's told Gisela, though, that most people don't practice this and that she should be very wary about sharing her abilities with others.

She has been meditating more and more recently, trying to hone a particular gift, as her Oma calls it, that lets her peer briefly into the thoughts and feelings of others around her.

She closes her eyes and concentrates. She focuses on the stale, warm air all around them, the feeling of each piece of clothing against her skin, and the slightly parched sensation on her lips. She pushes away the passing whim to drink some water and clears away all other straggling distractions.

Soon enough, her mind is completely blank.

She's been practicing this for months, so the process has gotten shorter and shorter.

Then, she zeroes in on Sophia, picturing her friend in her mind exactly where she sits next to her. She is leaning forward, hunched slightly, with her hand resting on her palm. Her doelike, dark brown eyes move rapidly as she reads something on her screen. Her right foot is tapping quietly against the carpeted floor, causing her midi-length skirt to swish gently and rub against the fabric of her chair.

Next, she concentrates on Sophia's mind—what she is thinking and feeling and pulls that energy towards her. In her head, it is like a ball of light blue light that floats away from Sophia's head and glides delicately into Gisela's palms.

From this whole endeavor, Gisela receives and interprets one strand of thought.

God, I really do want to leave this place. I'm just too scared to do it without a backup plan.

Gisela's eyes snap open and she takes in a few deep, silent breaths, one after the other. She slowly sits upright and wheels herself as close to the desk as possible. Then, she allows a smile to sprawl over her cheeks. *So there is hope after all,* she thinks, *I've just got to loosen her up a little and convince her.*

***

As Gisela is leaving at the end of her shift, she passes by Katherine's office. She pauses for a moment when she realizes the door is ajar.

Feeling confident from her recent success gathering Sophia's thoughts, she bites her lip and ducks her head into the doorway.

"Ms. Katherine?" she asks politely. "Are you busy right now?"

Katherine looks up at her from her desk, a mild alarm displayed on her face for half a second before she conceals it. "Yes, Ms. Schafer? Can I help you with something?"

Okay, I have to be quick, Gisela thinks. *Let's see how this goes.* Instead of taking the time to close her eyes and slowly focus on Katherine and her mind, she sharpens her thoughts with as much precision as possible to what she is feeling.

For a brief moment, a faint green glow outlines Katherine's figure, pulsing and disappearing just as fast. A wave of jealousy suddenly washes over Gisela, but not her own. *Katherine's… jealous of me?*

She blinks before offering her a small smile. "Just saying goodbye for the night. Have a nice evening."

Katherine raises an eyebrow and narrows her eyes; she peers at Gisela for a few seconds before frowning and letting out a long sigh. "Have a goodnight, Ms. Schafer," she responds with a tight voice.

Gisela nods and ducks back out before proceeding on her way.

As she leaves the gray and sparsely decorated office and opens the front door of the building to cool, brisk autumn air, she continues to ponder on her discovery.

"So that's why she targets me," she mutters to herself. She wraps her thick wool scarf around her neck and pulls her long trench coat tight around her body. She begins walking along the streets of Kreuzberg, Berlin, passing by many colorful individuals along the way. "If that's really her reasoning, there's no way she'll let up anytime soon," she continues, still talking to herself. "That's it then; I really do need to quit."

Chapter 2

Reward from practice

The air is brisk and light, filled with all the scents and promise of an autumn morning in Berlin. Gisela and her friend Mia are power-walking across Admiral Bridge, dressed in matching athletic wear sets in brown and beige. In these outfits, with their hair looped perfectly through the bands of their white ball caps, they look like fraternal twins.

The autumn reds and golds around them saturate the atmosphere like a brilliantly warm fire, making up for the chill in the air. There is some kind of gathering to the side of the wrought-iron bridge, where a few musicians stand in a tidy clump as a few dozen onlookers observe.

Some stand around them as they strum their guitars and begin singing in hushed, crooning voices, and others sit on the stone railings with their legs dangling and swinging in time with the beat.

Gisela glances over at them as she walks and can't help but smile. She recognizes the man singing as a local store owner who sells all sorts of knick-knacks, instruments, and tchotchke. There are also a few individuals she's seen time and time again walking about or hanging out on the bridge. They always dress in very whimsical, flowy clothing with bright patterns and floral prints.

All kinds of people fill the town with unique styles and quirks. Nobody really seems out of place or unusual; the town constantly buzzes with a magical and eclectic spirit. It's hard to explain without sounding a little silly to outsiders, but even the air around her feels alive. She grew up walking through these streets and often heard other locals saying they were all connected by the aura of the city.

Gisela has always felt a tiny emptiness deep inside, like something is missing from her life. Being a part of this community helps to quell that feeling just a little bit; she will never get over the wonder it instills in her.

"Pretty music," Mia remarks. She takes out her second earbud to listen fully. "Hey, don't we know that guy from somewhere? He looks kind of familiar."

Gisela turns to her and nods. The two of them slow down to a halt and turn to watch for a few minutes. "Yeah, he owns the little store a few blocks from here, The Lyre's Hamlet, I think it's called."

For a few more minutes, they stand and watch from afar, reveling in the fall-time euphoria around them. *Maybe I should try to get a little more practice in while I'm out,* Gisela thinks to herself. *Yesterday I was able to hear more than I ever have. I should keep that momentum going.*

She focuses on the singer, hoping that even though he is on the other side of the bridge, she'll be able to focus enough to get a glimpse into his thoughts. She shuts her eyes and takes a slow, deep breath; she knows Mia won't question it because she loves to soak in music thoughtfully and will probably think Gisela is doing the same.

Gisela is soon able to tune out the chatter and miscellaneous noise around her, honing in on the sound of strumming guitars and the melody being sung as it quickly swells. And then, she focuses on the singer alone, pushing past the words coming out of his mouth and thinking solely of his mind.

Soon enough, she visualizes a bright orb of energy in his head, clear and bright like a white Christmas light; it bobs and sways before floating ethereally into Gisela's open palms.

The man's thoughts barrel into her like a tidal wave, mingling with his strong feelings of contentment and bridled elation.

I'm so glad I picked up my guitar again, he is thinking. *I've been selling instruments for years now; I can't believe I'm just getting back to my love of music. Why didn't I listen to my brother sooner and join them out here? I'm never going back again.*

Gisela opens her eyes with a small gasp and tries to calm her heavy breathing and pounding heart. *Oh my gosh,* she thinks, *I've never read someone's thoughts and feelings at the same time before.* Reading a person's mind usually takes a bit of energy out of her, but never like this. Despite the sudden tiredness seeping into her bones, a sense of pride and satisfaction stirs within her. *I need some sustenance and fast.*

A little further down the bridge, someone is selling warm cider and apple strudel. The enticing scent of cinnamon and apple wafts by the two women, and as soon as they catch a whiff, they turn to look at each other with mischievous eyes.

"You don't have to tell me twice," Mia announces, already starting to head that way.

"I didn't even have to tell you *once*," Gisela barks with a loud laugh.

They hurry across the bridge and buy a cup of cider and a hot pastry for each of them. Gisela thinks briefly about trying to read the seller's mind too, but she decides to play it safe for now. *I don't wanna wind up passing out here in the middle of the bridge,* she muses. Then they continue their walk, warmth slowly filling their stomachs and spreading across their bodies as they dig into the food and sip at their drinks.

The filling in the strudels is gooey and perfect, with juicy, flavorful apples chopped to just the right size. As they pass over the rest of the bridge and continue toward the center of town, Mia moans with delight. Gisela grins at her before they make eye contact and both break out in laughter.

"I'm so glad we do this every week," Mia says, licking the rest of the filling off of her fingers before slinging an arm affectionately around Gisela and giving her a tight squeeze. "Even if today wasn't exactly the most effective workout."

"Well, you know, there's no way I could deny some hot apple cider," Gisela responds, "and trust me, your figure can handle it."

"Pshh!" Mia laughs, giving Gisela one more squeeze before pulling her arm away. "I'd say you're just flattering me, but I know you're the last person to lie just to do so."

Gisela smiles back at her affectionately and shakes her head. "You know me too well."

A few minutes later, they pass through one of Gisela's favorite parts of town. There's a painted mural stretched all the way across the wall of one building. The bright yellows, oranges, and greens offset the gray stone of the building across from it. Nestled in the center of the mural is a windowed door to a tiny local art gallery.

Feeling replenished and re-energized from her treat, Gisela decides to take this opportunity and try utilizing her gift once more.

"Hey Mia, wanna stop in here?" she asks. "I know the owner."

"Who don't you know around here?" Mia teases.

"Well, not many," Gisela replies. Her hand is already on the door handle, and Mia simply nods with a breezy laugh.

"We may as well. I think we finished our walk earlier anyway," she adds.

Gisela opens the door and they slide in as the bell above them rings softly.

"Oh, Gisela, so good to see you!" a man calls from the back of the building.

"Hey, Mario," she responds. "Where are you?"

"I'm in the back!" he yells. "I'll be out in a minute."

She and Mia stroll through the small, narrow gallery for a few minutes. There are about five rows, with just enough space in between to walk through. Paintings of all different sizes and styles line each one, bearing signatures from various local artists.

Shortly after, a short man wearing a newsboy cap strolls out from the back office and greets the two of them with a friendly smile. "Keeping warm, I hope?" he asks as he rubs his hands together. "It's starting to get cold out there."

"Trying," Gisela answers, holding up her half-empty cup of apple cider. "This is at least a little bit effective."

He laughs loudly and shakes his head. "Well, that's better than nothing."
He then turns towards Mia. "Is this your friend?"

"I'm Mia," she responds with a small smile. "We met at university."

"Nice to meet you, Mia. I'm Mario," he looks back at Gisela. "Now, I've
still got some things to do, but you girls just keep walking around as
much as you'd like, and let me know if you need anything."

I better do this fast, Gisela thinks. *I should try and see if I can at least get a reading
of his feelings, as I did with Katherine yesterday.*

She beams at him, all the while focusing her mind as intently as possible
within a couple of seconds. *Still your mind, Gisela.* She takes a small breath
in and clears all other thoughts away for just a moment.

Then, just briefly, she feels a wave of cheer rush towards her just as
Mario turns and walks away. She smiles. *Of course,* she thinks to herself. *I
don't think I've ever seen him unhappy.*

***

Gisela and Mia leave the art gallery just a few minutes afterward and walk
together to the closest point between their houses before saying
goodbye. She walks the rest of the way to her house, a two-story
townhome on the outskirts of town.

She walks across the small yet well-manicured green lawn toward her
front door. There are cornflowers and aster flowers lined on either side
of the sidewalk leading up to the patio, which has a swinging bench big
enough for two. She types in the passcode to her lock and it makes a soft
clicking noise as it unlocks. She lets herself in and heads straight to her
bedroom; she has to meet her Oma today, so she'll have to get showered
and ready quickly.

After a warm, refreshing shower, Gisela dresses in beige woolen
trousers, a fitted tank top, and a matching oversized blazer. Her
grandmother, who goes by the name Bast, likes to see her looking put-
together. Whenever Gisela gets ready, she reminisces on the one day she
showed up in a sweatsuit with no makeup on. Her Oma didn't say much,

but it was clear by the once-over and frown she gave her exactly how she felt.

So, Gisela sits down at her vanity and applies a light amount of makeup, and styles her long, brown hair in a claw clip.

The atmosphere of her bedroom always soothes her mind. Most of the decor is neutral and clean in appearance; her bed has cream-colored sheets and a huge, thick brown comforter spread across it, while her vanity and dresser are both ivory. There are fairy lights strung across her headboard and more hang down her closet doors, bathing the room in a subtle, golden glow. There are also little lamps shaped like stars on each of her end tables.

On another wall, she's hung up pictures of space in a variety of dark and colorful hues. They form a satisfying collage, made up of the black night sky dotted with a billion silver stars, bursts of a purple nebula, golden twin suns, and everything in between.

This room is her favorite part of this big house she inherited from her parents. The only thing her grandmother ever told her about them was that they adored space. So Gisela clung to that one little detail, subconsciously hoping it could bring her a little closer to the parents she's never known. Her bedroom simultaneously feels to her like a dawn shower and a galactic daydream.

Gisela finishes her routine and slides on some comfortable brown loafers before heading back out the door. The walk to Oma's house is short, only about ten minutes. She lives a little further out of town in a houseboat on the Landwehr Canal.

It is modest in size, yet luxurious nonetheless. Aside from the interior living space, there is a seating area on the top deck, complete with a hot tub and grill. *When has my Oma ever grilled anything?* Gisela wonders. *When have I ever seen her in the hot tub, for that matter?* She crosses the narrow dock onto the boat's front landing and knocks on the door.

The sound of clicking heels inside the house erupts from down the hallway, fast and sharp against the wood floor. In less than a minute, Bast swings open the door. Her willowy figure is as poised and elegant as ever, and her pale gray hair is swept up in a clean updo. Her short, wispy bangs stir with the rush of air that greets her.

Gisela instinctively stands up straighter as Bast's scrutinous eyes rake over her. "You're late," she finally greets tersely. Then she adds, "You look well."

Gisela nods and gives her a small smile. "Thank you, Oma."

Bast steps aside and gestures for her to come in. So Gisela walks through the entryway and heads straight towards the back of the boat to the meditation room. There is no door, only an open archway leading into it. Every wall is lined with slim floor-to-ceiling windows that allow the warm Berlin sunshine to pass through and illuminate the space in airborne golden hues.

Gisela hangs her bag on a hook right by the doorway and slips off her shoes before placing them on a small, woven shoe rack beneath it. Then she heads to a circle of cushions in the center of the room and settles down on the one furthest from the door. She tucks her legs beneath her as comfortably as she can and waits for Bast to arrive.

Shortly after, her grandmother enters the room, carrying a tray with two cups of warm tea. Her long, flowy dress swishes with every step. She sets the tray in the middle of the cushions and settles herself across from Gisela.

"So tell me, dear, how was this month?" she asks immediately. "How have you been coming along?"

"Well," Gisela says before gingerly picking up a steaming cup of English breakfast tea and sipping it slowly. "Work has been the same as it usually is. You know what my boss is like. Not much has changed in my life otherwise, either. As for my progress, though… well, you could say that's the only thing that has changed."

"How so?"

"I think you'd be proud," she adds. She lightly blows across her tea's hot surface before reaching with one hand for a spoonful of sugar and pouring it into the dark liquid. She stirs gently before taking an experimental sip. *Perfect,* she thinks.

"I'm so glad your tea is now *perfect* enough for you to continue," Bast quips with a raised eyebrow. "Now, do go on."

"Well, I've been able to hear others' thoughts much clearer lately," Gisela replies. "Just yesterday at work, I was able to hear the thoughts of my friend Sophia without any skipping or brain fog. Not only that, I think it's taking less and less time for my energy to recharge. Not long after, I was able to get a read on Katherine's feelings. It was the first time it's ever happened, but I felt an actual wave of emotion hit me when I focused on her. I think when I take less time to focus on someone, I read their emotions instead of their thoughts."

Bast nods. "Yes, you're coming along well. That's exactly how that works. With more practice, though, you'll be able to read both thoughts and emotions with minimal effort."

"Today, I listened to another person's thoughts while on my walk with Mia," Gisela continues with a smile, "and then I felt the emotions of the art gallery owner we know, Mario."

"Perfect," Bast says with a sigh. "It sounds like you've had an intense couple of days. Let's focus on some recharging meditation for today's visit. And afterward, I want to hear about your current hopes and dreams for the future."

"And maybe I can hear some more about your past and my parents after that?" Gisela pries, biting her lip.

Bast chuckles drily, but something indiscernible flashes in her eyes. "You know how I feel about those subjects," she answers with gentle rejection.

"Okay," Gisela sighs. "Maybe one day?" She takes another long sip of her tea and eyes her grandmother carefully.

Bast smiles and looks down into her own cup. "We'll see."

Chapter 3

A Dating Agency? WTF

For the next few days at work, all Gisela can think about is leaving her job. She's been itching to ask Sophia out for dinner and drinks but doesn't want to go into their meeting without a plan. So far this week, the only idea she's had in mind is to get a few drinks in her and loosen her up to the idea of starting their own business.

She has yet to come up with the most important part, and the part she knows Sophia would never overlook. What kind of business are they going to run?

Gisela has thought about starting their own marketing business since they have so much expertise surrounding the field already, but the idea doesn't excite her in the slightest. She's even thought about some kind of practice dealing with spirituality and meditation, where she could teach classes like her Oma has been teaching her her whole life.

I doubt Sophia would go for it, she thinks to herself as she sits in the break room at work, idly stirring around her salad with a fork. She likes to eat early, so not a single soul is in the room with her. *Besides, I haven't told anyone about the weird mind-reading thing. And I kind of doubt many people would be okay with it.*

She lets out a short puff of air before forking a big bite of ranch-covered lettuce and tomato into her mouth. The workday is not even half over and she already feels exhausted and defeated. Katherine has not let up on her since the other day; if anything, she's doubled down even more. In fact, whenever Gisela tries to get a read on her thoughts and emotions, they are so tangled and complicated that she can't figure out what's going on.

There's definitely still jealousy floating around, but also some frustration and anger. Her thoughts are so jumbled she can't hear anything coherent, but she thinks she's heard the name of a man thrown around in there. *Evan.* Every time she hears it, her own heart starts speeding up as if she's experiencing Katherine's own feelings.

I wonder if that's been the source of her frustration all this time, she muses. *Maybe she's just hung up on some guy who isn't giving her the time of day. Gosh, why are love lives so complicated but so interesting?*

Right then and there, Gisela stops eating. She shoves her fork into the salad with a satisfying crunch.

"Oh my god," she whispers to herself. "I've got it. I know what kind of business we should run."

***

After work ends that evening, Gisela is quick to pull Sophia aside and invite her out for drinks. She starts to hem and haw at first, talking about being tired and unsure if she wants to spend the extra money, and then Gisela offers to pay her way. Almost immediately, her "I don't know" turns into, "Well, if you're sure."

"I am so sure," Gisela sighs, looping an arm through hers. "I could really use this, actually. It's only Wednesday and we have to somehow make it through Friday. Come on, *please?*"

"Oh, okay," Sophia says with an eye roll and a wide grin. "Let me just run to the bathroom and freshen up. Then we can go."

"Oh, good plan," Gisela responds. "I could use that too."

They head to the office restroom and touch up their makeup lightly, adjust their hair, and mess with their clothes until they both feel satisfied. As soon as they leave, Gisela takes off her oversized blazer to reveal a high-neck backless bodysuit underneath, tucked neatly into her high-waisted leather trousers.

"Girl, you look hot!" Sophia exclaims. "You've been planning this, haven't you?"

"Maybe a little bit," Gisela laughs. "Come on; I know a nice little bar just a few minutes down the street."

"Oh, please tell me it's ERA," Sophia says, voice giddy. "I love love love that place."

"Well, now you've ruined the surprise," Gisela teases. "But yes, that is the establishment."

They link arms and continue strolling, relishing in the comfortably cool evening air and jovial ambiance of people milling about all around them. Just a block or two down from their office, ERA is already bustling as folks fresh from work show up in a variety of outfits, ranging from smart business attire like Gisela and Sophia to casual jeans or a short cocktail dress. Men in suits with undone ties are scattered across the sidewalk outside, clutching drinks and cigars.

As they get close, they can see the white and blue lights strung up over the entrance and the neon sign spelling out "ERA" in bold, slanted letters that are currently flickering at such a rapid pace it's barely noticeable.

There is something about this place that makes Gisela feel like she is stepping into another world. They push through the people bustling around the doorway and she marvels at the hundreds of white lights strewn across the ceiling inside. It feels like a swanky lounge nestled in the stars.

She is so focused on their surroundings, though, she doesn't notice the tall man in front of her currently trying to make his way to a table and collides with his chest.

"Oh!" she exclaims as she runs face-first into him. He inches back and places a hand lightly on her shoulder.

When his hand brushes her bare skin, she is too alarmed to bother looking up at his face or comprehending anything about his appearance.

A rush of warmth and a spark of static electricity slam through her skin all at once; the flaming heat seeps through her blood like molten honey, warming her up from the inside out. It rushes to her face and reddens her cheeks, and she gasps out loud at the intensity of these sudden sensations. Her fingers tremble and she struggles to catch her breath, but by the time she looks up to see him, he is gone.

She turns quickly around and catches a glimpse of his back as he vanishes into the swelling crowd. The dim lighting around them doesn't help. She does, however, notice his hair is long and either gray or some shade of blonde, and he is almost impossibly tall.

"Woah, get a load of that guy," Sophia huffs from behind her. "Come on, let's go sit at the bar."

"Y-Yeah, the bar," Gisela mumbles. *What is wrong with you? Get a grip,* she scolds herself inwardly. *Don't forget you have some serious social work to do tonight. You've got to get Sophia and yourself out of that job ASAP.*

They jostle their way through the crowd and towards the busy bar, and this time Gisela is hyper-aware of every person they pass. She subconsciously looks around to try and get another glimpse of the mysterious man from earlier, but so far, he is nowhere to be seen.

Thankfully, there are a couple of seats available at one end of the bar, with no room for anyone to sit beside them. *I can cram her into the corner and try to fend off any guys who come wandering. There's no room for funny business tonight.*

As soon as they sit down, the bartender approaches and takes their drink order. Along with their cocktails, Gisela asks for two shots of Malibu. Sophia looks at her with a raised eyebrow when he walks off.

"You do know we still have work in the morning, right?" She teases.

Gisela winks before laughing with her, and when the bartender brings over their drinks, they clink the shot glasses together and knock them back.

Hopefully, that won't be the case for much longer. Not at this job, anyway, Gisela thinks.

As they drink their first drink, Gisela starts gauging her friend's reaction to her ideas. "So," she begins, "have you given any more thought to what I said last week?"

"What are you talking about?" She asks, raising one eyebrow. "What did you say last week?"

"Oh, you know, I said we should leave our job and start our own business," she responds with a nonchalant shrug.

"Wait—you were serious about that?" Sophia asks, slamming her drink down. "Please tell me you're joking," she kids, but her voice is rising in pitch. "Oh, Gisela, I just don't know if it's a good time right now for that. Don't you think we need to stay stable right now while we can?"

She tries to pry into Sophia's thoughts the same way she's been getting a read on peoples' feelings. However, her lack of opportunity to focus for a long period of time, combined with Sophia's still guarded and alert mentality, makes it more than difficult to do so.

"You don't need to freak on me," Gisela eases, lifting her free hand in surrender. "It's just an idea. I just know you hate the place just as much as I do. And if I'm honest, I've been feeling really tired and restless lately. I just thought maybe you'd like a change of pace too."

"I mean, come on," Sophia says with a heavy sigh. The bartender comes over to interrupt and Gisela quickly orders another round of drinks. "You know I do," she finally finishes after he walks away.

"Well, good!" Gisela exclaims with a laugh. "Let's do it then. We're probably the most competent people we know. We can do it."

"I still don't know," Sophia huffs. The bartender places a dirty Shirley Temple in her hands and she sips on the straw with a sudden eagerness.

"Well, just think about it," Gisela says. "Just promise me you'll consider it?"

Sophia shifts in her seat, and by her slower, more relaxed movements, Gisela can tell the liquor is loosening her up. She tries once again to pry into her mind.

A warm orange aura radiates over her body, tinged by a faint pink hue underneath. Then a wash of nervous excitement sweeps over her, and she can't control the hopeful fluttering of her heart.

Oh my god, she really wants this, Gisela thinks eagerly. She shifts in her seat and takes in a deep, measured breath. *Now I have to actually convince her.*

"What would we even do?" Sophia asks, shaking the ice around in her already half-finished drink. "Like, what kind of business are you talking about?"

"Okay, hear me out," Gisela murmurs. She can't even keep the excitement out of her tone now. She leans closer. "I thought of this earlier today."

"Well?"

"We should open…" She pauses to beat out a drumroll on the bartop. "A dating agency!"

"A… dating agency?" Sophia questions. Confusion flickers in her eyes for a few moments before giving way to something more positive. "Wait… for real?"

Gisela nods slowly. She can't contain the huge smile as it spreads across her face. She's feeling warm herself from the alcohol flowing steadily through her. "For real."

"Oh my god, that actually sounds amazing," Sophia says slowly with a shy smile. "Do you really think we could pull that off? Wait, wait, what would I be in charge of?"

"Well, you'd be in charge of the business and financial side of things. I know how great you are with numbers and management."

"Aww, thanks," Sophia laughs and tosses her braids over her shoulder. "You know, I've really been wanting more responsibility and more of a challenge lately."

Gisela nods. "I know it. And you would be amazing at this. I would take care of the clients more one-on-one and work on the personal side of things. I've just been thinking lately about how much people fascinate me and how interesting it would be to work with them like this."

"This really does sound great," Sophia sighs as she leans back and finishes her drink. She smiles contentedly and looks away in thought.

Gisela tries one last time to pry into her mind.

This time, even with just a brief amount of concentration, she discerns one floating thought. *There's no security there, though. What about the future? What about a backup plan?*

Gisela sucks in a breath and reaches out to touch her friend's hand. "Come on, Soph, do you really want to spend our thirties still stuck in an unfulfilling job? We still have time. And worse comes to worst, we have work experience to find another job pretty fast, and I have a huge house you can crash in whenever you need."

Sophia bites her lip and looks back at her with furrowed brows.

"Oh, what the hell," she finally exclaims. She sits up and reaches out to shake Gisela's hand; she clasps it eagerly and flashes a huge grin in return. "Let's do this."

"Ma'am," the bartender interrupts. Gisela turns around and he passes two tall glasses of bubbling champagne in their direction. "A gentleman at the end of the bar wanted to send you these. He didn't want you to know his name, though."

"Oh!" Gisela slowly pulls hers over and peers into the glass. She looks over across the bar but doesn't recognize anyone there. "Well, tell him thank you for us, please."

"He's left already, I'm afraid," he says with a small smile. "And he's paid the rest of your tab."

"Holy crap," Sophia says with a burst of laughter. "Looks like tonight was meant to be, huh? Let's cheer."

Gisela holds up her glass with a small smile. "To us," she agrees with a nod.

"And to getting out of that hellhole and away from Satan herself," Sophia adds with a snort. They clink their glasses together and each takes a long gulp.

I wonder if it could be my mystery man? Gisela muses. *Just what is he playing at?*

Chapter 4

New alliances

The next day at work, Gisela and Sophia are both a bit harried and hungover, yet full of nervous energy and excitement at the same time.

After drinks last night, Sophia went home with Gisela so they could rest up and continue plotting. They stayed up late talking, laughing, and eating snacks like teenagers.

Today there is an executive meeting where Katherine and the marketing department will meet and talk with some of the higher executives about plans for the new quarter and progress updates. It's at this very meeting they will make their move, effectively handing over their resignations and humiliating Katherine in one fell swoop.

As soon as the handful of executives from other branches and headquarters arrive in the office, Sophia's leg starts bouncing with unease. Their voices carry all the way down from the front entrance down to the end of the building as Katherine greets each one.

Gisela looks over at her friend, who's currently rolled back from her desk to peer down the hallway and biting her nails. When she focuses on her for a moment, the same orange aura from the night before glows around her frame and a wave of anxiety floods through Gisela's system. *Note to self,* she thinks, *don't read Sophia's feelings when she's clearly nervous. I don't need any extra nerves of my own.*

"Don't worry," she soothes, "we'll be okay. I can do all the talking if you want."

Sophia nods and looks over at her. "Are you sure?"

"Yeah, all I'm going to do is say something about how Katherine wastes time and productivity picking through all of my work and documents when we have a perfectly capable editing department to catch any mistakes. And then I will say something about her being jealous because I know that will really get to her. Then you and I will get up and hand our resignation letters to her personally before leaving the room."

"Okay, okay," Sophia mutters, taking slow, long breaths. "I think I can handle that."

"Good," Gisela says with a smile as I rest my hand on her arm. "I'm sure Katherine will be here any second eager to breathe down our neck about getting over there, so we might as well go now."

They make their way to the conference room, where Katherine and the executives are just starting to set up the meeting. Katherine flashes them a tense (and clearly fake) smile as they find their way to their seats. She never displays her usual aggression towards them around the other executives.

When everyone has been seated and the company CFO begins the meeting, Gisela realizes one crucial detail.

The man sitting across the table from Katherine has a name tag; he is none other than Evan himself.

Well, well, well. Look what we have here.

She listens intently for the main duration of the meeting as each executive takes a turn going over business plans for the next quarter. Still, this new development is continuously brewing in the back of her mind, like a simmering pot of bisque left on low heat. She tries to contain the smile that wants to bubble up to her face. Finally, she figures out the perfect way to utilize this information.

Eventually, it comes time for Katherine to talk about their branch and what kind of work has been done there; she opens up a folder and begins to read aloud about progress and productivity. She briefly mentions Gisela and Sophia by name, claiming animatedly that they are both excellent assets for their workplace—which they are.

"I love my marketing team here," she says with a wide grin, looking over where Gisela and Sophia are seated. The two of them share a glance.

Just like every other meeting, Gisela thinks with a barely audible groan.

Finally, it comes to the point in the meeting she's been waiting for.

The CFO, John Müller, clears his throat and looks toward them with a warm smile. "Anything to add, ladies?"

"Well, I did have some points to bring up after Katherine's very kind words," Gisela responds with a tense smile of her own. "In fact, I have to say that she isn't being entirely truthful about her love for us."

"Is that so?" he asks.

Katherine stares at them with barely narrowed eyes; her fists clench and her jaw tightens, but Gisela knows she wouldn't dare say something antagonistic in front of the others.

"Well, to be honest, Mr. Muller," Gisela continues, "Ms. Katherine seems to visit our office about twenty or so times a day to chastise us. You see, while those productivity numbers are good… they could be great."

"Please continue," he says with a nod, leaning forward and folding his hands together on the table.

"I feel that Ms. Katherine has been letting her… well, I'm not sure exactly, but I have a feeling it's jealousy… get the better of her. She spends her hours picking over every single piece of work me and Miss Sophia here produce. When we make so much as a single mistake on a form, like the date, or a typo that could easily be caught by our very skilled and professional editing department, she brings it to our attention and wastes this company's valuable time by forcing us to do the forms over entirely."

He leans back and looks over at Katherine from the sides of his eyes. "Is this true, Ms. Katherine?" he asks, his voice low and dry.

"Well, sir, I—"

Gisela stands suddenly, and Sophia hastily follows. "I'm sorry to interrupt, sir, but she has actually made the atmosphere for us around here just very sour and unpleasant. Not only does she nitpick our work, but she degrades me for having autism almost daily, even though I am one of the most productive workers in the office. I'm afraid me and Sophia, from this day on, will be taking our leave of the company. Thank you for giving us this opportunity; we have our resignation letters to give to Ms. Katherine now."

"Actually, *I'll* take them," he answers tersely. His shoulders strain against his jacket and his gaze refuses to linger on Ms. Katherine any longer. "I'm very sorry to see the two of you go. Is there nothing I can say to sway your mind?"

"I'm afraid not," she answers with a frown. "But I appreciate the notion." They walk around the table and pass their envelopes to him. Gisela pauses at the doorway to the room and looks back over her shoulder to glance between Katherine and Evan. "Oh, and Katherine, maybe if you let go of some of that pent-up bitterness, Mr. Evan over there would actually spare you a glance."

Her reaction is immediate and excruciatingly satisfying as her entire face blooms with redness to rival a chili pepper. Her hands are now visibly shaking, and she hastily tucks them away beneath the table. Gisela can't contain her smirk any longer, and she glances toward Evan to see his dark eyes widen and his brows crease.

She gives one final nod to the executives around the room before turning back around and leaving.

***

That night, Gisela and Sophia celebrate with another drink at the bar; they even call up a few friends to invite out with them, including some of their college buddies. They decide to go back to ERA, not just because they both love the ambiance but also because, in the back of Gisela's mind, she is hoping to catch another glimpse of her mystery man.

Sophia even teases her on the way over, not knowing how truly impacted she feels by their encounter, saying they might end up with another round of free drinks.

Gisela's childhood friends, Monika and Jurgen, are already there when they arrive, along with a mutual friend she and Sophia went to college with named Hans. He happens to run a startup tech business with Jurgen, so he's well acquainted with him and his sister. They've staked out a table in one of the back corners closest to the bar.

Their other friend from college, Klaus, walks up behind them as they veer toward the table and greets them both with a warm smile.

"Hey, everyone," Gisela says with a grin as she sits beside Monika. Next to Monika is her brother Jurgen, with Hans on his other side. Klaus settles in beside Hans and the two simply greet each other with a complicated handshake.

"Hey!" Sophia shouts with a huge grin as she sets her bag on the empty seat next to Gisela. "First round's on me!" She throws her hands up with a cheer and the sounds of glee echo around them as everyone else joins in. She hurries off to the bar and Gisela watches with interest as Klaus stands up to follow, mumbling something about helping her carry them.

"So," Monika says with a sly smile as she looks at Gisela. She nonchalantly flips her dark, wavy hair over one shoulder and raises an eyebrow. "Finally ditching that place and striking out on your own?"

"You bet," Gisela says with a nod. "Did Sophia tell you what kind of business we're starting?"

"No," Monilka answers with narrowed eyes. Her curious smile grows wider. "What kind of business are you starting?"

"A dating agency," she replies with a firm nod. "I wanted to do something where I could be more involved with people, one on one. Something where I could really analyze and look at their quirks."

"Absolutely," Monika says with a breezy laugh. "That sounds just like you. So is Sophia going to deal with the numbers stuff then?"

"Yes, ma'am," Sophia responds jovially, carrying a tray in her hands filled with cocktails and tequila shots. They jostle slightly as she moves, ice clinking against glass. For a moment, Gisela debates leaping up to help, but Klaus follows closely behind her.

He is holding a tray of his own, loaded with tall glasses of beer. Still, he reaches out with one hand to stabilize Sophia's arm when the tray starts to tip.

As time seems to slow down between them, she glances back at him, surprise lighting her eyes. Gisela watches for a moment as an indescribable zip of energy buzzes between them.

The moment ends quickly, and Sophia turns away to set her tray down on the table. Eager hands slide forward to grab drinks and shots while Klaus arranges beers in the middle.

"You know, I would love to help you guys out with marketing," Monika continues. "I am the advertising manager in my office, after all. Of course, I would do it on the house for my bestie," she finishes, giving Gisela a playful wink.

"That would be amazing," Gisela answers with a wide grin. "I'd love to talk some more about your suggestions too. I'll take any advice you have."

"You should visit Jurgen and Hans sometime, too," Monika adds. "I'm sure they could help you out with the tech side of things."

"Okay, sit, sit, everyone," Jurgen urges. "I'm ready to get this party started. Let's make a toast."

Sophia and Klaus hastily sit in their respective seats and everyone picks up a shot glass before raising them in the air.

"To Gisela and Sophia," Jurgen proclaims. The large ring on his right hand clinks noisily against his shot glass; its multicolored stone glistens like stardust in the dim bar lighting. "And to starting something new," he continues, "prost."

"Prost!" The rest of them shout, clinking tiny glasses together and throwing them down with haste. Five glasses hit the table all at once, and Sophia and Gisela look at each other before bursting out in excited giggles.

Hans shakes his head and smiles before sharing an amused glance with Jurgen. Klaus laughs along with them, the smile lines around his warm eyes wrinkling. Gisela looks over at him and realizes his gaze is locked on Sophia. She smiles silently to herself and takes a long sip of her Long Island iced tea.

As the commotion calms down, the group starts to break off into separate, quiet conversations while everyone downs their mixed drinks. Gisela listens intently to her friends, eager for any opportunity to peer into one of their minds.

When she focuses on Monika and Jurgen, she hears something especially interesting.

"Don't you think this will be great for the Collective?" Monika murmurs to her brother.

"It definitely could," he responds. "Let's talk about that later, though."

Gisela blinks and looks up at them. *What in the world is the Collective?* She wonders. She takes in a deep, quiet breath and focuses her energy on Monika for a few moments before reaching out to her mind.

Almost immediately, a dark gray wall slides up in her head, completely blocking her from reading Monika's thoughts or feelings.

She grips the seat below her and tries to calibrate; it feels as if she physically ran into a stone wall, and her head is pounding with the onset of a headache. *What?* She runs a hand through her hair and shakes her head. *What does* that *mean?*

When she looks at Monika, it seems like she is doing anything she can to avoid eye contact. Her jaw is tight as she talks to Hans and Jurgen, and even though she is speaking normally, something seems off.

"Hey, what are you thinking?" Sophia asks. Gisela turns and notices her friend eyeing her with concern.

"Oh, not much," she replies, trying to brush off her lingering confusion. *I'll table this for now.*

"I'm just so excited," she whispers to Sophia, leaning close enough for her hair to brush against the mahogany skin of her shoulder.

"Me too," Sophia whispers back. She links her pinky with Gisela's and presses her head to hers. "I was really nervous about all this at first, but now I really feel like we might make it."

"We will make it," Gisela affirms. *Why am I even bothering with trying to read anybody's thoughts right now?* She thinks. *I should just focus on the here and now. I'm actually going to do this.* "Just watch."

Chapter 5

Suitable digs

Over the next few days, Gisela and Sophia start to feel the nerves and antsiness from leaving their jobs kick in. Sophia has been staying with Gisela in one of her guest rooms so they can communicate at all hours, and each day has been a whirlwind of brainstorming and writing.

After just three days of being cooped up, they've already filled two notebooks worth of ideas and objectives.

Even though Gisela feels secure and excited about the goals they've come up with, she's eager to start taking solid steps. All this time staying inside has her itching to just *do* something, so one morning, the two of them make plans to meet up with Monika and Mia for breakfast.

After rising early, unable to sleep with all the thoughts whirring around her brain, Gisela takes her time to get ready. She completes the longer version of her luxurious skincare routine, applies a full face of makeup, and styles her hair in a slick braid. She dresses herself in a comfortable knit sweater and loose-fitting trousers, and when she is finally done, it is only 8:00 a.m.

Then she empties out the large, beige Marc Jacobs tote bag she previously used for work and fills it with the notebooks she and Sophia have filled out, an empty one, a budget planner, a regular planner, and her laptop. Just as she fits the last odds and ends they might need during their outing, Sophia knocks on the door to her at-home office and smiles broadly at her.

Her thick, curly hair is moisturized and defined to perfection; it reaches just past her shoulders. She is wearing a pale pink bodysuit and cream-colored trousers that complement her dark, glowing skin with a dreamy softness.

It seems like neither woman will be ditching her workwear wardrobe anytime soon.

"You ready?" she asks Gisela. "I am hungry for some quiche." She rubs her stomach dramatically. "And mimosas." She wiggles her brows.

"You're so right," Gisela answers with a groan. "I am so sick of takeout and pizza. Let's go get a real meal."

She slings her now-heavy bag over her shoulder and they head out.

***

They meet up with Monika and Mia at a local diner just near the outside of town and join them at a round table outside. The weather is mild and pleasant, slightly warm with a gentle breeze. The two brunettes have already ordered mimosas for the four of them.

"Hey, girls," Sophia greets. She gives a quick hug to both Mia and Monika before she and Gisela sit down.

"Monika was just telling me all about your plans," Mia says with an open smile. "I am so, so excited for you guys. Oh my gosh! A dating agency? That is so cool!"

"Thanks!" Gisela responds. "We're really excited. We have a lot of plans in here." She gestures to her tote bag as she sits down and hangs it on her seat. "Two notebooks' worth. But we've been itching to get some concrete plans in action."

"Yes, and we thought we knew just the two ladies to help us get the ball rolling," Sophia added.

Monika raised a brow and gave her a smirk. "I've been *dying* to talk to you two about your marketing plans since drinks the other night," she admitted. "I think this is going to be amazing. And I already have some strategies mapped out for you."

"Good!" Sophia continues, barely missing a beat. She pulls out her phone and says, "I already started social media accounts, but we need help growing them."

"Done," Mia interrupts. "I'm going to write some articles for you to post online. Just send me your details, mission statement, brand vision, and whatever else you need to. I'll type something up to put out there on the station's website and then I'll talk to my boss about shouting you out on air."

The waitress comes in between their talking to take everyone's food order, and in between drinking mimosas and chatting, Monika starts writing out detailed marketing schemes.

The buzz of reciprocity, friendship, and productivity hums in the air around them. All four women wear broad smiles and flushed cheeks throughout the whole meal as they play off each others' excitement and knowledge.

By the end of breakfast, Gisela and Sophia walk away feeling completely relieved of their mounting stress. Still, one more thing is left on their agenda.

As they walk arm-in-arm and newly carefree through the streets of Berlin, Gisela remarks, "We still need to find an actual building."

"That we do," Sophia responds. Just before they leave Kreuzberg, she directs them down an unfamiliar side street. "Which is why I've been researching new listings the past couple of days."

"You have?" Gisela asks, mouth gaping. "How did you find the time?"

"Girl, it's not like I've been sleeping," Sophia laughs and smacks her arm. "Just wait until you see what I've found."

Gisela bites her lip and narrows her eyes. Curiosity buds and blooms in her stomach as the nervous excitement hums in her fingers. The space around them seems to open up as a narrow alleyway widens into a bustling downtown street. The brick is made of red and brown cobblestone, warm and inviting, and all around, vendors are set up hawking their wares.

The smell of cinnamon and fried foods wafts through the air like a tantalizing trail, and customers dressed in fashion-forward looks mill about toting bags of handmade goods, festival food, and colorful drinks.

Things smothered in powdered sugar, honey glaze, fruit, and spices surround them with a cacophony of scent and color.

"Have you brought me to a fair?" Gisela asks, eyeing Sophia with genuine interest. "I'm not sure how this will help the building situation, but it could inspire us."

Sophia chortles. "No, silly. Although, this is definitely a pleasant surprise… and maybe even a good omen."

Gisela reaches out to Sophia's mind and, to her surprise, realizes her friend is being completely sincere. A sense of hopefulness glows around her in an amber mist. It fills Gisela's own spirit with joy.

They pass through the bustling street, Gisela guided by Sophia's steady hand, and she marvels at the lovely brick buildings all around them. The street's very atmosphere seems to beckon her closer.

A few blocks later, Sophia stops them in front of a charming, white brick building with tall windows all along the front wall. A for sale sign is plastered against the white wooden door.

"Here it is," Sophia whispers. Gisela can tell by the quietness in her voice she is even more pleasantly surprised than she expected to be. "It's even prettier than in the pictures."

"Wow," Gisela coos. She steps towards the windows and peers inside. The entrance room is mostly empty, save for a few floral arrangements littered around the wooden surface and floorboard. "What's with all the flowers?" She brushes her hair back and looks behind her at Sophia.

"Well, it used to be a flower shop," she responds, taking a step forward, "but the owner is moving, so she wants to sell it to someone new. She said online she's really hoping it will go to a young entrepreneur like she once was." Her eyes sparkle. "But maybe she's willing to go for a couple of young entrepreneurs."

Gisela laughs softly. "That… would be amazing." She takes a step back and looks up. Every nerve and sense of anxiety quiets within her as perfect calm takes its place.

Is this the place for us? she wonders. She finds herself hesitating to take the leap, yet can't think of a single reason why not.

Finally, she looks over at Sophia again, this time with a smile.

"How soon can you get us in touch with the owner?"

Chapter 6

Flowers blooming, hearts fluttering

It turns out they aren't able to get the owner of the building on the phone until a few hours later. Their first call, placed while standing in front of the old flower shop, is met almost immediately with a voicemail message from the owner. A woman named Aria, who sounds to be somewhere in her forties, lets them know she won't be available until 1:00 p.m.

They find themselves back at Gisela's house and spend their time walking around the living room, biting their nails, and scrolling through their phones. Every now and then, Gisela gets a burst of creativity, so she starts making rough sketches on her tablet of what the interior of their agency could look like. Of course, it's a little bit difficult to imagine it precisely when they haven't seen the building's full interior.

Even the soft, ivory-colored throw blankets and neutral furniture can't calm Sophia down. She gets up from the sofa every so often to pace and intermittently scribbles hasty notes in a folder. Gisela suggests they eat some lunch to pass the time, but her friend claims she is too nauseous to get anything down.

So they wait.

The minutes tick by like slow-moving slugs on their phone screens and Gisela's tablet. Still, they wait.

At around noon, Sophia gets the idea to look up the building online to try and find some more pictures. They wind up at the now-closed flower shop's business page, filled with lovingly written notes and descriptions, as well as clearly professional photos taken of the space.

The whole area is lit with sunlight during the day, thanks to the tall windows at the front of the store. Carefully curated flower bouquets and arrangements blanket every surface and seem to glow under the sun's golden glaze.

There are a couple of open-brick walls and a few separate rooms, including office space, storage, and a bathroom. Probably one of the building's best features is the all-glass office space near the very back. Gisela's heart expands in her chest when she looks at it, and Sophia must see the delight written all over her face because she smiles at her and murmurs, "That room is yours."

They spend some more time browsing the website before looking for another distraction. Sophia starts to look over Gisela's rough design plans and re-work them to better fit the building's layout.

By the time 1:00 p.m. rolls around, Gisela has changed into a tank top and bike shorts and opted to keep the blankets far away. The overhead fan is running on high to keep up with her nervous sweats.

Finally, Sophia calls Aria one more time, and the call goes through.

"Good afternoon," the woman greets. "May I ask who I'm speaking with?"

"Yes! Good afternoon, ma'am. My name is Sophia." She pulls her phone from her face to put it on speaker. "I'm here with my business partner, Gisela. We left you a voice message earlier. I wanted to inquire about the building you've put up for sale on Liebesstraße."

"Oh, yes, my old flower shop." There is a note of wistfulness in her voice. "Ladies, I'm afraid I am incredibly selective on who I choose to sell this building to. I'm not sure we're going to come to an agreement."

Gisela and Sophia exchange a worried look.

"I understand that, Ms. Aria," Sophia eases. "The building is very beautiful. Me and my partner found it today and we knew it would be the perfect place to start our business. I can assure you, we're very passionate about this project."

For the next few minutes, it feels as if they are talking in circles.

Aria is reluctant and fussy; it's clear there is something holding her back. She keeps backtracking during their conversation, bringing up reasons why she *shouldn't* sell it to them.

Every time, Gisela or Sophia offers a rebuttal to her worries. They talk about their reliability, their savings, and their own lives to try and get Aria to open up to them.

"I just really want to make sure this building is going into the right hands," Aria declares. "I mean, it's so special to me, you know? This shop… it was everything to me." Her voice is heavier now, almost sad.

"Ms. Aria, believe me, we know," Gisela cuts in. "It was a very special shop. We could tell just by looking at your pictures online and the building in person. It carries its own radiance. It already feels special to us. I can't imagine how special it is to you."

"Well, yes… you understand." The woman lets out a sigh over the line. "Maybe I'm just projecting my own doubts onto you sweet girls. Moving is… scary, you know. I've lived in this city so long, and even though I know it's time to go home, I still don't feel ready." She pauses. Gisela can't help but wonder why she refers to where she's moving as home already.

If only I could read her feelings over the phone.

"Now, you said you're starting a business?" Aria asks. "I really would prefer my place to go to somebody like you ladies. Someone with a creative, entrepreneurial spirit. It would be wasted on anything less. What kind of business are you looking to start?"

"A dating agency," Sophia answers. "We really want to create a beautiful, warm place for people to learn more about themselves and others. And, of course, make their very own love connections. Wouldn't it be so fitting to be in a place that used to be a flower shop?"

"Well, actually," Aria murmurs, "I suppose that is fitting…" she trails off before muttering something under her breath.

Gisela leans closer, and she swears she catches something along the lines of, "benefit the Collective."

How odd, she muses. *The Collective? Didn't Monika say something like that the other night?*

Sophia is biting her fingernails and looking over at her with wide, brown eyes. They wait with bated breath for a few more moments.

"Okay," Aria finally says, voice louder and firmer than it's been for the whole conversation. "I'll sell you the building. If you like, we can work out some kind of payment plan, and I'll send over the appropriate documents this evening so we can begin the official process." She pauses. "This will be good for us, anyway…" she trails off again, her voice seemingly distant.

Gisela hears her whisper something else about aiding a "Collective," and can't help the senses of bafflement and curiosity building simultaneously within her.

"I'm glad to have met you two ladies," Aria resumes abruptly, "and perhaps one day our paths will cross in person. Have a good night."

"Goodnight, Ms. Aria," Sophia rushes. "You will not be disappointed. Thank you so much!"

As soon as they hang up, Sophia looks at Gisela with still-wide eyes, but they carry a much different expression.

"Ahh!" she yells. Gisela grins back at her before pulling her friend into a tight hug.

"We did it, Soph!" she squeals.

"We're doing it! We're doing it!" Sophia breathes. "Thank you so much for convincing me to leave that job. I couldn't ask for a better friend."

Gisela squeezes her with renewed firmness. "Of course. Thank you for believing in us."

***

After their phone call, they have too much energy built up in their systems to stop moving, so they whip up a quick lunch at Gisela's house and get back to work.

Sophia texts Aria to ask her for some more pictures of the building, and they receive some almost immediately. Since Aria is currently out of the city, she is unable to meet with them in person. However, she lets them know over text that she can arrange for a family member to drop off the key as soon as the paperwork is signed.

They decide to move their work to Gisela's desktop computer and get started on the building's new design. Gisela brings an extra chair upstairs to her office, and they sit side by side at her desk.

They browse through furniture shops for inspiration and a few key pieces, make plans to stop by some consignment stores, and put together a cleaner version of Gisela's sketches.

As they are finishing up listing out the items they'll need to purchase, Sophia starts tapping her fingers restlessly on the desk's wooden surface.

"Something on your mind?" Gisela asks as she saves their design file once again.

"Well, I was just thinking about the fact we don't actually have a budget planned out yet," Sophia admits. "That's kind of an important step."

"Yeah…" Gisela trails off. "This is why I'm glad I have you," she teases. She tosses a glance at her friend, who gives her a small smile.

"Really, though," Sophia insists. "We should get on that. We can't just go spending money willy-nilly without some kind of game plan."

"You're right." Gisela nods. She reaches out briefly to get a sense of Sophia's feelings, and a pale orange glow floats around her frame. There is a layer of joy and excitement that grazes across Gisela's heart, but it's carried by an undercurrent of fear.

"I know just the person to consult," Gisela adds. She would be lying, too, if she wasn't excited to see Sophia interact some more with the very person who could help them. "Let me call up Klaus."

***

A few hours later, the two women feel more satisfied with the prospects of their careers than they ever have.

Aria has corresponded with them more via email, and they've already filled out the proper paperwork and sent it back over to her. Every little step seems to bring them that much closer to what could be the life of their dreams.

They're on their way to a contemporary steakhouse just a few blocks down from Gisela's house, where Klaus is already waiting. With some encouragement from Gisela, Sophia borrows a lovely midi-length satin dress; its shimmery gold fabric hugs her figure to perfection. Gisela smirks to herself as her friend eyes her reflection.

"You look gorgeous," she remarks.

"Thanks, girl," Sophia replies. Gisela notices the soft blush across her cheeks. "Do you think…" She trails off.

"Yes, I think Klaus will think so too," Gisela quips.

"Gisela!" Sophia squeals, eyes going wide when she turns to her. "Quit!"

Gisela throws her head back and laughs. "Oh, come on, I'm just teasing," she replies.

To throw her off her scent, Gisela dresses up as well. It's a fairly upscale place, after all, and she'll take any opportunity to show off her well-curated evening wear. She opts for an A-line tea-length dress in a deep burgundy color that accentuates her honey-colored hair. She sweeps her hair quickly into an updo just before they head out, and the two are on their way.

They walk to the restaurant, relishing in the cooled air against their bare arms. When they arrive, they are greeted by a dark and intimate atmosphere. There are candles and subtle neon lights littered throughout the building, and just by the entrance, a live jazz band croons soothing, gentle music that floats across every room.

They find Klaus already seated at a booth towards the back of the restaurant, skimming his eyes over the pages of a book-style menu. He looks up as they approach, and Gisela notices instantly how long his eyes linger on Sophia.

"Ladies," he greets as they approach. He stands up, and they see he is wearing a neat and trimly tailored suit. The only thing messy about him is his medium-length, light brown hair that hangs in waves around his chin. It's parted down the middle like usual, and somehow he manages to make the messy look seem polished.

"Klaus, hello!" Gisela greets. She gives him a loose side hug before taking a seat across the table.

"Hi there, Klaus," Sophia adds, her voice soft.

That's uncharacteristic of her, Gisela thinks with amusement. *This must be a sign that our starting a dating agency is a good plan.*

"You look gorgeous," he continues. "Both of you." His eyes, however, are still on Sophia.

"Thank you," she stammers. She quickly straightens herself in her seat and holds her chin high. "You clean up nice, Kliss Klaus."

He lets out a deep chuckle and shakes his head. "Never change, Soph," he responds affectionately.

Gisela met both of them in college—separately—and pulled them each into their burgeoning friend group. She could swear that ever since she introduced them, he's been making googly eyes at Sophia. Meanwhile, Sophia seems to have been oblivious up until this very moment.

Maybe it was sooner, Gisela muses. *Maybe I've been too caught up in my own inner world to realize what's been going on with my own best friend.*

"Speaking of college nicknames," she interrupts. "I'll never forgive you two for the worst one yet."

"Oh, *Gissy* dear!" Sophia taunts, crinkling her nose and erupting in bright, tinkling laughter. "Don't fret!"

Gisela mimes herself barfing and rolls her eyes, but a broad smile fills her face.

Klaus watches in amusement before laughing himself. "It's so good to hang out again, just the three of us," he says. "And I wanted to again congratulate you two on starting this new venture." Just at that moment, a waiter brings over a bottle of champagne. He pours it generously into each of their glasses. "I want to propose a toast," he continues, "to new adventures." They lift their drinks. "And to the two of you."

"To us!" Gisela and Sophia reciprocate. They glance at each other before clinking glasses and taking long sips.

"So," Klaus proceeds. He sets down his cup. "We're here to talk business. Tell me; how can I help?"

They pass the dinner by amiably, with good conversation and even better food. Gisela orders a filet, Sophia orders lobster, and Klaus himself orders a NY strip. All the while, Klaus helps them set up a secure financial plan for their business in the coming months. The two women make notes on their phones and he emails them digital documents for licensing and opening up a business bank account.

Gisela watches the whole evening as playful banter passes back and forth between him and Sophia. The softness in his blue eyes when he looks at her is endearing—almost as endearing as the bright pink aura that radiates around both of them whenever she focuses on their feelings.

She harnesses her powers somewhat sparingly, though, because she feels so swept up in the moment and in their energy. She can feel herself filling up with gladness and excitement, not just for the coming months but for the flower blossoming before her very eyes.

Chapter 7

Oh my gosh: Life and love

After dinner with Klaus, nearly everything about the agency feels settled. The morning Gisela receives their new key from Aria's sister, she and Sophia head over to the building to begin preparations.

The street has calmed down since their first visit, but the warm early morning breeze and calm ambiance of people walking quietly down the road gives the area a different kind of charm.

There is a pastry and coffee cart set up just a block away from the building, so they stop by and pick up some hot treats to renew their energy before going on. When they arrive, the sunlight is so beautifully playing along the storefront windows that Gisela's breath is nearly taken away.

When she turns to look at Sophia, she doesn't need to read her thoughts to know she feels the exact same way. Still, for the sake of practice, she focuses acutely on Sophia's mind. It takes much less time than usual, and Sophia's thoughts bubble up to the surface like boiling water with ease.

It looks so beautiful in the light, Sophia thinks, *I can't believe we're actually doing this. It feels so perfect... so right. I know this is where we're meant to be.*

Gisela pulls away and smiles warmly at her friend, who is still staring in awe at their agency's new residence.

"You know," she says gently, "there's one thing we still haven't decided on."

"Yeah?" Sophia looks at her. "I can think of several things we still need to decide," she teases before asking, "What?"

"A name," Gisela answers softly. She looks back at the building. "Got any ideas?"

"Nope," Sophia answers, shaking her head. Her black curls bounce in time with the motion. "You?"

"I…" Gisela hesitates. "I think so."

"Well, spill!" Sophia urges. She grins and takes Gisela's hands in her own. "I'm hopeless in that area, girl. Tell me."

"Okay," Gisela says slowly, smile widening. "How about Leben and Lieben?"

Sophia squeals softly. "That's so cute! Life and Love… I adore that. L and L for short, maybe?"

"Perfect," Gisela breathes. She can feel a tension she didn't know was in her chest loosen and release. "I think that's great. Wanna head in?"

"Yes! Let's go!" Sophia links her arm in Gisela's. "I can't believe this is real. Can you?"

"Hardly," Gisela admits. "Yet at the same time, I couldn't believe us doing anything else."

They approach the door together and she watches Sophia as she unlocks and opens it. When they walk inside, the lovely view is instantly disrupted by a billow of dust that floats up and consumes their faces.

"Oh my gosh!" Sophia exclaims, coughing and fanning wildly around her face. "How long has this place been closed?!"

"I thought it was only a few months!" Gisela responds. She ducks and fights the itchy buildup overwhelming her throat. She coughs a few times and hobbles further into the room. "She probably hasn't been in here once since!"

The entrance space is rather small; it seems to have served as some kind of lobby or display area at one point. There is a wall that separates it from the rest of the space, and through the doorless entryway, Gisela can see the all-glass office she fell in love with on the website.

"You think we can knock this wall down?" Gisela asks, looking over at Sophia. "I don't know a lot about renovation, to be honest."

"I know a little bit," she replies slowly. She walks up and brushes a hand across the wall's surface. "My parents renovated their house when I was a teenager, and I helped out a little."

"So, in other words, you probably know much more than you'll let on," Gisela teases.

Sophia's face flushes and she lets out a short, high-pitched laugh.

"You always sell yourself short," Gisela continues more seriously. She backs away from the wall before continuing into the rest of the space. "I'll leave the reno part mostly in your hands," she calls over her shoulder.

"Yeah, yeah," Sophia shouts back, but there's a hint of pride in her voice. Gisela knows in most projects like this, it's best to stand back and let her take the lead. Sophia can be a bit perfectionistic, but it's something she highly admires about her.

She wanders around the mostly empty space. There are a few old cans and empty flower pots, as well as several wilting flower bundles and dead plants. The office space is completely empty except for a sleek, minimalist desk built of light birch wood. She swipes a finger down the length of the glass door, lifting a line of dust from its surface.

"There's definitely enough cleaning to be done in here," Sophia announces as she follows in Gisela's footsteps. "Aria could have at least picked these flowers up when she left it." She pulls a brown and curled-up leaf disdainfully from a clay pot. Her nose crinkles with disgust. "How about I get started on the wall, and you handle this stuff?"

Gisela turns and looks back at her. Her mouth twists in amusement. "Sure thing," she says. "Looks like we've got ourselves a deal."

They begin to work in comfortable quiet; after Sophia picks up some things from her house and a nearby supply store, she lays everything out on a white towel. Meanwhile, Gisela disposes of every dead plant and empty tin and sets aside the freshly cleaned vases and pots.

"Wanna come smash this wall with me?" Sophia asks, peeping around the corner at Gisela as she dusts the last square inch of her office wall.

Gisela halts her sweeping motion and turns to her with a wicked smirk. "I thought you'd never ask."

She drops her duster and practically skips over to Sophia.

"Okay, first put on these geeky goggles," Sophia says with a giggle.

Gisela raises an eyebrow but dutifully takes the pair of clunky, clear goggles and slides them down over her eyes.

"They're kind of loose," she complains. She can feel her skin itching incessantly; she hates the feeling of loose things that are supposed to be tight.

Sophia nods and quickly steps around behind her and effortlessly tightens her goggles. As the rubbery material cinches securely against her face, Gisela can feel herself instantly relax. The itching stops.

"Thank you," she breathes. She smiles at Sophia and picks up one of two sledgehammers. "Let's do this thing."

Sophia grins and picks up her own. "You take that side; I'll take the other."

Gisela nods and shifts the hammer's weight experimentally in her hands before looking up at her friend.

"You take the first strike," Sophia says with a nod. "If it weren't for you, we wouldn't be here."

Gisela can feel her eyes moisten. She reaches her mind out for just a moment and feels a brush of love and admiration oozing off of Sophia. It fills her heart all the more until she feels like her whole being is alight.

She pulls the sledgehammer back and swings.

The first blow crashes satisfyingly into the wall with a booming crunch, and as plaster and drywall crumble around it, she lets out a shrieking laugh.

"Oh my gosh!" Sophia yells, erupting in laughter as well, "that was so damn cool." With haste, she lifts and swings her own hammer before smacking it with force into the wall. They laugh and grin at each other as, swing by swing, the wall before them collapses and falls to pieces around their feet.

Somehow, Gisela thinks to herself, *smashing this wall feels more than literal. I can't wait to break down all the barriers that once stood in my way.*

***

A few days later, Gisela and Sophia set aside some time to step away from the renovations and meet up with Hans and Jurgen. They've agreed to meet them at their base of operations to talk about a potential business partnership.

Since their building, which it turns out is more like a warehouse than an office, is almost an hour's walking distance, they decide to hitch a taxi and ride over there. On the way, Gisea begins briefing Sophia on their meeting.

"They're both highly knowledgeable about the tech world and the industry as a whole," she tells her. She shifts in the uncomfortable taxi seat to look at her friend. Sophia eyes her inquisitively. She's holding a few folders of her own and Gisela's tote bag full of journals and notes sits between them.

"You're sure about that, right?" Sophia asks slowly. "I mean, I know Hans has a degree in this field, but..." She trails off. "They are just a start-up, and we'd be their first major client."

"But not their *first,*" Gisela points out. "And I've known Jurgen and Monika since childhood. He's always been a whiz with computers or really anything involving technology. He's probably the smartest person

I know. Don't let his social awkwardness throw you off, though. He can be pretty blunt and sarcastic."

"Oh please," Sophia teases with a roll of her eyes. "I'm used to dealing with you, after all. I'm sure I can handle him."

Gisela laughs loudly and shoves her shoulder. "Wow!" she exclaims. "Maybe you are a match for him, actually. Watch out, Jurgen."

Sophia giggles and crinkles her nose. "Whatever," she replies, voice light.

"Anyway," Gisela continues through her laughter, "He's very intelligent. And they have worked with some smaller, short-term clients before." She reaches into her bag and pulls out a manila folder before opening its contents for Sophia to examine. "This is a detailed report of all their previous and ongoing projects, as well as an analysis of each of their experiences with the tech industry."

"That's really thorough," Sophia says slowly. She traces her fingers over the stack of papers and skims quickly through the first page before looking back at Gisela. "I trust you," she adds with a small smile. She gently closes the folder. "I'll be open."

"Thank you," Gisela says with a nod. She slides the folder back into her bag before quipping, "That report took a long time; you could have at least read a couple of pages."

Sophia snorts and sticks her tongue out at her, and the two women erupt in muffled laughter.

Before too long, they arrive at the facility. There's a metal sign hanging over the front double doors that reads, "Hans on Tech."

"Wow, that name is really… something," Gisela remarks as they step out into the street.

Sophia glances at her with raised brows. "'Something' is right. Clever? Maybe. Funny? Not so much."

Gisela huffs out a short laugh. "I'd say they were going for funny."

"They missed the mark," Sophia kids.

"Don't let their poor joke-telling ability ruin your opinion of them already," Gisela teases as she loops her arm through Sophia's and pulls her towards the entrance. "Come on; I think they're waiting."

They walk through the front doors and are immediately greeted by Hans. "Ladies," he says with a nod. He brushes a few strands of short, dark hair away from his forehead. "I was just about to meet you outside. Come with me."

"Oh, okay," Sophia responds, blinking rapidly. She shoots a look at Gisela, who simply smiles back. Hans is already turned around and walking briskly down the hallway.

From what they observe from the building's interior, the decoration is minimal at best, with a slight touch of industrialism. There are open brick walls, metal beams along the ceiling, and a few rustic-looking tables here and there. The lighting, however, is bright and cool, which feels jarring against the otherwise warm elements of design.

As they walk for a few minutes through winding hallways, they come to an open lobby of sorts, with two different pathways leading away from it.

There is a large, golden archway draped with a heavy curtain on one side, with no hall. The curtain itself is a work of art and possibly the most interesting thing she's seen in their building so far. The fabric is a dark forest green, woven with faint intricate designs.

There are oddly shaped trees, small creatures, and rivers that wind in between. When she narrows her eyes to peer closer, she notices tiny symbols reminiscent of an ancient language.

She wonders at the meaning and symbolism of it. *It looks nothing like anything I've ever seen,* she ponders. Her curiosity is helplessly piqued. She's never seen anything so enticing.

Hans stops at a door across the room and begins keying something in on the keypad. Sophia watches him intently while Gisela continues to marvel at the mysterious archway.

"What's in that room?" she finally asks. When she looks back at Hans, he is observing her with cool, unreadable eyes. "Could we see it?"

"I'm afraid that's confidential," he answers quickly, "but I'm sure Jurgen would be happy to show you around the rest of the building after our meeting."

"Do you two have something to hide?" Sophia asks, crossing her arms. Her tone is teasing, but her face is serious. "That's not exactly the best first impression."

Hans smirks. "You haven't changed a bit since college," he remarks. "And I hope you'll understand. We simply have private documents and instruments being used or created for our current projects. We're only protecting the privacy of our clients."

"Oh," Sophia answers with a nod. Her face flushes slightly. "Well, maybe it is a good impression."

"Glad to hear it," Hans replies. He opens the door with a *whoosh* of air and gestures for them to step inside. "Ladies first."

Sophia tilts her head at him before laughing and walking inside. Gisela follows slowly after her. She looks up at Hans for a moment and considers reaching out to feel his thoughts. Yet a small feeling of trepidation stops her from doing so.

Why is my intuition telling me something is off? She thinks. *Hans is a friend. He can be trusted. Still, Oma always told me to listen to my gut. And my gut is telling me not to pry right now.* She meets his emotionless stare with her own before giving him a smile and a nod.

"Thanks," she says, breathless. She doesn't realize she'd been holding her breath until she walks into the room.

"Gisela!" Jurgen greets from across the office.

She doesn't have time to ponder on her strange feelings any longer because when she turns around, Jurgen is approaching her with open arms.

"Long time no see," he kids as he pulls her into a quick squeeze. "It's so good to sit down and meet with you to talk business. This is Sophia, your partner, right?" He turns towards Sophia and grins. "I believe we met briefly the other night?"

She smiles back. "Yes, we did. Sort of. We didn't really get a chance to interact much."

"What a shame," he replies. It's hard to miss the quick once-over he does of her with his eyes. "What a pleasure to make your acquaintance, Miss Sophia. He holds out his hand and when she places her own within it to shake, he instead slips it into a lax position and swiftly presses a kiss to her knuckles.

"Oh!" Sophia exclaims, her face reddening. "Nice to, uhm, meet you, Mr. Jurgen." She glances at Gisela, eyes screaming, *"Help,"* but Gisela stifles a laugh behind her palm.

Jurgen smirks at her and slowly releases her hand. "Me and Gisela were childhood friends," he continues, "along with my sister, Monika, who you've met. I'm excited to meet yet another one of her college friends." He looks at Gisela now with a jokingly stern expression. "I just wish she hadn't kept *you* from us for quite so long."

Sophia's cheeks flush an even deeper scarlet and she clears her throat with a nervous laugh. "You sure know how to charm," she kids. She seems to collect her bearings for a moment before straightening and giving them all a huge smile. "I say let's get started, right?"

"Yes, let's," Gisela agrees.

The office is spacious but sparingly furnished. One side of the room is lined with two large, antique wooden desks mounted with desktop computers on separate walls with black leather office chairs. There is a long, dark oak table that runs almost the entire length of the room in the center, lined with sleek metal chairs in brushed bronze. At the other end, a coffee bar and a potted ivy in the corner complete the office.

Jurgen directs them towards the conference-style table and they each take a seat, Jurgen and Hans on one side and them on the other. Jurgen slides his laptop in front of himself and opens it up before positioning it so they can all view it.

"I've been looking over the documents you sent us," he begins, "and we have plenty of ideas to share with you." He and Hans dive straight into their prepared demonstration, flipping through slides on the computer and skimming over spreadsheets and charts as Gisela and Sophia watch with wide eyes.

They listen closely to their spiel about technology and the software needed to run a highly efficient, eventually large-scale agency like L and L. They even talk about their proposed ideas to structure the matchmaking database and a way to effectively log and keep track of every client's information.

Hans emphasizes the importance of security and gives a short, well-delivered speech on data encryption that Gisela only barely comprehends.

By the end of their speech, she and Sophia have to sit and process everything they've said in utter silence.

"Well," Sophia finally says with a short laugh, "I'm impressed."

"Yeah," Gisela agrees, "I can't say I followed along perfectly, but I really enjoyed the way your vision for our company aligns with our own."

"And don't simply give us this contract just because of our friendship," Jurgen urges. His smile is teasing, though. "I won't turn down the advantage, though. But I truly believe no other company will be able to serve your needs like our own."

"Like 'Hans on Tech' can?" Sophia teases. Gisela looks at her and almost bursts out laughing, but she manages to stay composed.

"Exactly," Hans says seriously.

"Hey now, don't put down our name," Jurgen jokes. "We worked hard on that." His eyes flash with amusement. "And I can promise you, I'm a hard worker in all areas of life." Gisela can't help but notice he barely peels his stare away from Sophia through the whole exchange.

Her friend practically squirms under the attention, and although she seems mildly flattered, when Gisela reaches out for her feelings, a wave of confused tension comes off her in waves.

"Alright," Gisela interrupts. She clears her throat and watches in relief as Jurgen turns his stare back to her. *Jurgen has always been charming, but this fixation on Sophia seems... intense.* "Let's talk numbers. Have you got a contract for us to sign?" She pulls out another folder from her bag. "Because we've got one for you."

***

After they end their meeting with contracts signed and payment plans in order, Gisela and Sophia walk out of the building feeling a mixture of relief and dismay.

Almost as soon as they're outside in the evening air, Sophia asks, "Am I the only one who thought they were a little bit... weird?"

"No," Gisela responds immediately, "it was definitely strange the way Hans talked about that room. But I think it could just genuinely be best business practices they're trying to follow. And Jurgen... well he's always been kind of odd. And Hans is really quiet, as you know," she nods at her, "but there is a different side of him when it comes to business, I suppose."

"I guess so," Sophia says slowly. When Gisela reaches out to her mind, she can feel a mild sense of trepidation hanging around her. "Now that we're out here, away from all the overwhelming jumble of words and technological jargon... I just hope we didn't rush into this, is all."

"I understand," Gisela agrees. She rests a hand on her friend's shoulder. "But I think it'll be okay. These men are just a bit odd, nothing more. I believe they'll help our business thrive. Besides, I wanna talk about something much more interesting..." She trails off and smirks; from the look on Sophia's face, she knows exactly what this is about.

"Oh, hush!" Sophia squeaks. "I don't even wanna think about it."

"Two suitors calling after you in, what? A week?" Gisela snorts.

"I wouldn't exactly call them suitors," Sophia mutters. She shakes her head and looks at Gisela with dismay. "Would you?!"

Gisela slings her head back and chortles. "Maybe, maybe not. But both Klaus and Jurgen seemed pretty keen on you when we met up."

"Well, I didn't really mind the way Klaus was acting," Sophia responds shyly.

Gisela clutches her arm with excitement. "That man has been pining after you since college!" she cheers. "Oh my gosh, is my favorite pairing finally going to happen?"

"Hold your horses," Sophia laughs. But she can't contain the wide smile across her cheeks.

"Holding," Gisela jokes, holding up her hands as if she's grasping at reins. "But wait; how'd you feel about Jurgen's flirting, then?"

"I'm not sure," Sophia admits with a frown. She brushes her curls behind her ear. "I mean, he seems really nice. But something about his attention was a little off-putting. I mean, he doesn't know me and he was just… a little *too* focused on me. He wouldn't stop staring into my eyes like he was trying to hypnotize me or something."

Or read your mind. The thought flits through Gisela's mind like a passing car, sudden and fast. *Wait a minute… could he? Could he have some abilities like me?* She furrows her brow. *I guess it isn't implausible.*

"I don't know if I want a relationship anyway, to be honest," Sophia continues, snapping Gisela away from her contemplation. "This business is going to take most of my time up, and relationships take work."

"That's true," Gisela agrees, "but I'm sure if it's right, it will work out. And to me, at least, Klaus is looking *pretty* right."

Sophia giggles. "Alright, alright! I get it. I'll think about it, okay?"

"That's all I can ask," Gisela responds in a singsong voice.

Just then, their taxi pulls up, and the two women pile into the back. Sophia seems calm now, but on their drive back, Gisela can't halt her own worried thoughts.

There definitely was something off about Hans' behavior, she thinks. *I just hope whatever it is doesn't bleed into our business relationship.*

Chapter 8

Romance is in the air: Snap

As the weeks continue to pass in a blur of renovations, shopping, painting, decorating, and working closely with all their friends to set the gears of Leben and Lieben in motion, Gisela can feel her heart and hopefulness continue to swell as well.

Monika and Jurgen arrive at the building one afternoon to help set up their computers and phone lines, but after everything has been configured, Monika reveals she has another surprise up her sleeve.

Gisela sits at the desk in her all-glass office; its surface is tidy and minimal, but every bit and bob she could possibly need is organized to perfection. She has a vase filled with flowers she refreshes at least once a week. Thankfully, Ms. Aria has offered to provide them with free florals until her remaining inventory runs out. Every time Gisela looks at her desk, a rush of serotonin floods her veins.

Sophia is currently sitting beside her with the rolling chair she's pulled over from her own office, and Monika leans between the two of them to pull up something on the computer. Meanwhile, Jurgen stands behind all of them and watches with a confident smirk.

"I know me and Mia have been the ones keeping track of your social media and I've been handling the majority of your marketing," Monika says, thinly veiled excitement in her voice, "and we've been pretty much keeping you in the dark. But I wanted to show you the fruit of our efforts."

"Okay, show us," Sophia teases. "You've successfully pulled me to the edge of my seat."

"Well…" Monika trails off. She's typed in the address for Instagram now, and as soon as it loads, she logs into Leben and Lieben's page. "What do you think of five hundred thousand followers?"

"Five hundred…" Gisela breathes. "Thousand… *what?*" She sputters, and her heart flutters rapidly in her chest. "You're joking, right?"

Monika navigates to the business profile, and the follower number reads "523.6k."

"Numbers don't lie," she chimes.

"Oh my god!" Sophia squeals. She turns to Gisela with eyes the size of saucers and a gaping mouth. She grabs Gisela's arms and shrieks. "Gisela, *look!*"

"I see, I see!" Gisela gushes. "I just… wow, I can't…" She struggles to catch her breath as tears prick in her eyes. She looks up at Monika, who's standing up straight with crossed arms and a casual smirk. "How did you two do it?"

"Well, I've been working my butt off running sponsored ads for you up the wazoo," she replies. "Plus, you may be featured on a couple or a few billboards and in the ad spaces of some local newspapers. And Mia has been amazing too. She wrote some local interest pieces on a couple of news sites and even got her managers to agree to let her give L and L a shoutout on air."

"She did?" Gisela springs up from her feet. "Oh gosh. I need to thank her." She turns to Monika. "I need to thank you!" She yanks Monika into her arms and the tall brunette gives her an awkward pat on the back.

"No worries," she replies.

"I need to call up Mia and get her here," Gisela continues. "You guys have done so much for us."

Sophia stands as well and straightens her blouse. "You're right. I'll call her. Why don't you go out and put some thank you baskets together or something like I'm sure you already plan on doing."

Gisela laughs and smiles at Sophia before reaching for her hand and giving it a squeeze.

Suddenly, the bell above the building's front door tinkles brightly. When Gisela and Sophia exchange confused looks, Monika murmurs, "One step ahead of you."

"Guess who's here!" Mia shouts from the entryway. "Your favorite blonde!"

"And me!" Klaus adds. Somebody mumbles something. "And Hans!"

"Oh my gosh," Sophia gasps. She looks at Monika. "Why are they—"

"They're all here to help with the finishing touches of L and L," Monika answers before she can finish. "And speaking of baskets… me and Mia actually prepared one for you two."

"Well, now I definitely need to make one," Gisela kids. She hurries out of her office and everyone except Jurgen trails behind. He mentions something about double-checking the programs on her computer before they're out the door.

"Mia, hi! Hey Klaus; hey Hans!" Gisela piles into Mia's warm hug with fervor before looking at her with a tender grin. "I'm so happy to see you. Thank you so much for everything. Monika showed me our Instagram."

"Oh, I'm just so happy I could help make your big dreams come true." Mia shyly tucks a strand of hair behind her ear. "And so happy to just be here, along for the ride."

"Special delivery," Klaus interrupts. He sets a large basket brimming with sparkling tissue, candy, snacks, and mini bottles of wine on an empty table. "For…" He makes a show of looking at the handwritten tag. "A Ms. Gisela and Ms. Sophia. 'Make a toast for us, to the future. Love, Monika and Mia.'"

"Aww," Sophia gushes, hands clasped at her chest. "You guys," she draws out her words, and when Gisela looks at her, affection is clearly brimming in her eyes. "You didn't have to do all this. Thank you."

"We wanted to," Monika adds as she walks over. Her hands are tucked casually in the pockets of her gray trousers. "After all, what are best friends for?"

"The bestest," Gisela says with a smile. She looks between all her friends and quickly reaches out to as many feelings in the room as possible. Everybody's aura radiates brightly with hues of green, pink, and violet. She feels surrounded by joy and color in the best way possible. "Alright, best friends," she continues, clasping her hands. "We've still got furniture to rearrange. Let's get to work."

***

The six of them work quickly and efficiently, arranging furniture until it is "just right" in Gisela and Sophia's eyes, unloading boxes, and hanging leftover paintings and pictures on the walls.

About halfway through their work, Gisela decides to tear into her gift basket and allow everybody to indulge in the snacks held inside. She slips away to buy some water and sodas from a nearby store. When she returns, she totes it all to a little break room in the back, where the men have set up a fridge and a table with chairs. Klaus is currently working on installing a sink when she walks in.

"Thank you so much for that," she breathes. He reaches over to open the fridge for her and she passes him a small smile. She unloads all the beverages inside before taking a water bottle for herself. "Help yourself to anything in here. I've just bought some water bottles and a couple of kinds of soda."

"Thank you, Gisela," he replies. "I've just about got this sink hooked up, and then this room will be good to go."

"I'll have to buy some soap and paper towels," she muses. "Thank you again. I appreciate all of your time. I know you don't have a plethora of days off work, so it means a lot you would use some of your free time to come here and help."

"Oh, it's really my pleasure," he assures her.

"You know…" She trails off and leans against the fridge with a smirk on her face. He looks up with a furrowed brow. "I know who else probably really likes having you here." She watches with delight as his expression softens and color flushes to his cheeks.

"Oh yeah?" he asks. He coughs and looks back down at the sink. "Who's that?"

"Sophia!" she exclaims.

He starts and looks up at her with wide eyes, only to see her grinning at the door.

"Hey!" Sophia exclaims with matching enthusiasm. Her lips and brows quirk with befuddlement. "Why are you acting like I didn't see you just two minutes ago?"

Gisela laughs and steps away from the fridge so she can get a drink. She pops open the tab on a can of Coke before taking a long chug.

Klaus stands up and wipes his hands on his jeans. "All done," he proclaims. His eyes land on Sophia and Gisela beams as she watches the smile lines fold around them. "Hi, Sophia. I didn't really get to talk to you yet."

"Hey, Kliss Klaus," she replies with a soft smile. "Thank you for coming here today. It's good seeing you again."

"I love your outfit," he comments. She's wearing a pair of pale, blush-colored linen pants and a breezy white blouse. "You look radiant."

"Aww, thanks," she says with a gentle laugh. Her cheeks are already starting to glow. "You're not too bad yourself. It's not often I get to see you in jeans."

"It's not often enough I get to see you," he replies in an instant. "We really should get together sometime."

"Yes, we all love seeing Ms. Sophia," another voice adds from the doorway.

Gisela turns and watches with curious amusement as Jurgen leans against the doorframe. He steps into the room and saunters toward them.

"Jeans are certainly comfortable." He glances at Klaus. "I can tell, Sophia, you value style a bit over comfort, like yours truly."

"A little presumptuous, don't you think?" Sophia asks with a raised eyebrow. "I'm actually very comfortable right now. But thank you… I think."

"I should thank you," he quips. His eyes rake over her and he runs a hand back through his cropped dark hair. "For the view."

Gisela looks with widened eyes between Jurgen and Klaus; she notices Klaus visibly stiffen. He crosses his clenched hands behind his back and forces a tight smile. She doesn't have to read their minds to know what anybody is thinking.

"Well, Sophia certainly offers more than just a 'view,'" Klaus interrupts. "She's quite brilliant."

"Boys, boys," Sophia laughs. She waves her hands. "I think it's time for this brilliant view to escort herself back into the lobby."

Just as she finishes talking, Mia peers into the room. She looks around at them all for a moment before entering. Gisela flashes a warm smile before saying, "Come join the fray, Mia."

She blushes and quietly shuffles towards them, her eyes cast away.

"I don't believe you two have met," Gisela says to Jurgen and Mia. "Jurgen, Mia. Mia, Jurgen. You know what Mia does, Jurgen. Mia, Jurgen here runs the startup tech company we're partnering with alongside Hans. He's been setting up our programs for us on the computers."

Jurgen slowly turns around and as soon as he looks at Mia, all the worry Gisela had fostered about his rivalry with Klaus vanishes.

Something in his pale blue eyes almost sparkles. "Yes, the reporter," he breathes. All the charisma and slyness seem to evaporate from his being.

Mia looks up at him with a nervous smile and throws her long, blonde hair over her shoulder. "The techie," she replies quietly. "Nice to meet you."

"The pleasure is mine." He gathers his bearings quickly and tenderly reaches for her hand. Everyone watches with bated breath, and it feels as if the air has been sucked out of the room. He raises her hand to his mouth and presses a small kiss against the underside of her wrist.

Mia's pupils flare at the gesture, and her mouth forms an 'o' as she stares, speechless.

After a few moments, he slowly drops her arm and she clears her throat. He turns away and scratches the back of his head.

That's the most awkward thing I've ever seen him do, Gisela muses. *I don't think I've ever seen him act so humble.*

"I just wanted to tell you two," Mia begins, voice breathless. "I just got word from my boss that I'll be allowed to cover your grand opening when it happens. You and your building are going to be broadcast live for all of Berlin."

"Gisela!" Sophia gasps. She grabs her hand. "Mia! Oh my gosh! That's amazing!"

"It's *so* amazing," Gisela agrees. She pulls Mia towards them. "Thank you. Truly. We couldn't be here without friends like all of you."

"Guess you better start opening up applications and sending out invitations," Mia continues. "Soon enough, you're gonna be open for business."

Chapter 9

Mysterious snippets

The next day, Gisela must meet with her grandmother, Bast; she's already pushed their monthly meeting back because of her work on Leben and Lieben, but she hasn't actually told Bast about her new business yet.

As she sits and partakes in tea and pointed small talk in the meditation room, she mulls over the fact she'll have to come clean sooner or later. Judging by the passive-aggressive looks and disdainful quiet that have been filling the air since she arrived, sooner would be better.

"Well, I'm glad you could finally make time in your oh-so-busy schedule to come to see your poor, lonely Oma," Bast drawls as she stirs a bit of honey into her tea. She looks up at Gisela, whose own cup contains thrice the amount of sweetener, and raises an eyebrow. "Your hair is messy, by the way. Haven't you been oiling and brushing it before every wash like I told you?"

Gisela self-consciously fingers her hair. *It doesn't feel that messy to me,* she thinks, but she knows to bite her tongue. "Yes, Oma," she responds dryly. "I think your eyesight is starting to fail you in your old age." *Well, I guess I can only bite it so much.*

Oma chuckles and takes a long sip of her tea. "That's my girl," she rasps. "You truly are... just like your mother."

Gisela perks up at this. "My mother?" She breathes, her heart starting to beat. "Are you finally going to tell me about her?"

"Hold on, now, child," Bast chides. "One thing at a time." She slowly sets her teacup down on its plate. "First, tell me what you've been keeping from me."

Oh, great. I should've figured she already knows, Gisela thinks. "I do have some news," she admits, "and I think you'll be excited about it. You should be. I am."

"Go on, spit it out. I hate babbling."

"Me and my friend, Sophia, have started a business together."

"A business? What kind of business? And what happened to your other job?"

"We left," she adds. "We've been working hard on setting up our new building. We bought it from a lady named Aria, who used to run a flower shop inside it."

"Oh, Aria," Oma says with a smile. "I know her. She was… interesting. A very creative spirit, for sure. A little eccentric. She had the tendency to, how should I say this? Buck traditions."

"Were you two close?" Gisela asks, barely hiding her surprise. *It's not like Oma to speak as if she knows someone so well.*

"Not really," she says with a slight shrug. "I guess you could say we grew up in the same neighborhood together. Many of us knew her."

Us? Gisela wonders. *I guess she must mean the other kids in the neighborhood.*

"Anyway, what kind of business are you starting?" Bast presses. "Do you think it will be viable going forward? How close to opening are you?"

"We're actually planning a grand opening just next week," Gisela responds. "And yes. I think it is already very viable. Monika and Mia have been working hard to get our name out there, and we already have hundreds of applicants lining up to come to our opening night. I think I'll have to turn some away." She chuckles. "There's only so much we can keep up with."

"That's all very good, but you didn't answer my first question," Bast snaps with narrowed eyes.

"Oh! I'm sorry, Oma." Gisela laughs and opens her mouth with hesitation. "It's called Leben and Lieben. We're opening a dating agency."

Bast suddenly stills. "A… dating agency," she murmurs. Her pale eyes look far away, and she sips thoughtfully at her drink while Gisela waits with bated breath. "Yes… that could be very good. Very good for the Collective."

There it is again! Gisela straightens with alarm. "Collective?" she asks immediately.

"Oh, well, you know. The general Collective of Kreuzberg," Bast answers with a wave of her arm. "I was merely thinking out loud. Don't mind my musings."

"So… what do you think?" Gisela queries.

"Yes, I think that could be very good. You and Sophia are partners?"

"We are," she answers with a nod. "She will handle most of the logistical and financial side of the business, and I will manage the social side. I'll analyze our clients and work with them personally to find the right match."

"It sounds like you're finding your true calling finally," Bast observes. For the first time today, she gives her granddaughter a gentle smile. "Your mother would be proud."

"Now that I've answered your questions," Gisela blurts out, "will you tell me about her?"

Bast clicks her tongue and smiles wider in amusement. "Not so fast. You know we need to do our meditation first. Speaking of which, this could also be a good opportunity for you to work on your abilities, my dear. Take advantage of that."

Gisela nods. "Sure, Oma. I will."

For a moment, doubt flickers in Oma's eyes. "Although," she starts, voice low, "just be careful, alright? Don't get too close to any of your clients and tell them about your family."

"Why not?"

"Well, just… you never know who will sign up. It's best to keep your personal life private. Trust me."

"Okay…" Gisela answers. Yet she can't help wondering, *why the sudden change in tone? What exactly is she thinking?*

They continue from here to go about their usual meditation practices, and this time Gisela is able to quiet her mind with absolute ease. In just a moment, she brings herself out of her own thoughts and into a state of pure silence. She feels her consciousness float about herself like a drifting balloon; it's as if she's left her body entirely.

For a few minutes, she observes herself and her Oma from above.

Oh my god, she thinks. A strange thrill of excitement shoots through her.

As she watches, Bast opens her eyes and stares intently at her body.

"Gisela?" she murmurs.

Gisela opens her mouth to speak but can't bring herself to. *I don't know if she'd even hear me.*

She watches as Bast reaches towards her and gently presses her hand against her face. For a second, pain flashes, undeniable, across Oma's features. She mouths out a few words Gisela can't discern.

She moves closer until she is almost touching her own body. *Does Oma know I'm here?* she wonders.

She watches as her Oma closes her eyes and continues mouthing soundless words. The shapes she's making with her mouth are unfamiliar, though, like she is speaking in a foreign tongue.

I wonder how she is feeling. She looks so… distraught. I've never seen her walls down like that. Gisela had never tried to read Oma's feelings before; she always made it clear those powers were strictly off-limits with her. *But she can't see me now.* Her heart starts thrumming wildly in her chest, but it feels far off. *I'm surprised I can still feel anything from my body right now.*

She pushes down the growing unease and reaches out to Oma's mind.

For the briefest instant, a pale cloud of gray floats about her presence.

And then, like a trap ensnaring a mouse, Bast's face snaps in her direction. Gisela's blood runs cold. Her Oma's pale eyes are now stormy as they stare straight into her, and one thing is for sure: she is livid.

Just like that, Gisela's being floods back inside her body, and she awakens with a deep gasp. It feels as if her lungs have been storing up breaths, and now she must breathe through all of them in a few seconds. She clutches at her chest and hunches over, gulping raggedy bursts of air.

"It takes a toll on your body the first couple of times you shift," Bast drawls. Gisela listens as she picks up her cup of tea and takes a short sip. "Once you've caught your breath, you may excuse yourself."

"But, Oma, I'm sorry! I—"

"Leave," Bast repeats, cutting her off. "I told you never to use your powers on me. You need to learn how to listen."

"But my mother," Gisela blurts in desperation. "You were going to—"

"Now!" She interrupts. She practically slams her tea on its plate and unfolds her legs to stand. "You seem like you're breathing well enough to argue. You can go." Without waiting for another word, she walks out of the room.

Gisela is left to shakily bring herself to her feet and hold her stomach as the tears bleed freely from her eyes.

***

Gisela heads home that evening feeling distraught and dismayed; her mind is a whirling vortex of thoughts and confusion. She is wondering how in the world she will ever distract herself from that meeting with Oma when her phone lights up in her hand.

A notification fills the screen to let her know she's received a text.

> Sophia: Would you meet me at L and L in a few minutes? There are just a few last-minute touch-ups we need to do.

She sucks in a deep breath and halts in her tracks. She clutches her coat closer to her body; the nighttime air is even colder than usual this night. *Well, there's one distraction,* she muses.

She chews her lip for a moment before sending a quick response.

> Gisela: Be right there.

Then she tucks her phone into her coat pocket and turns around to start walking that way.

In just around twenty minutes, she finds herself in front of Leben and Lieben but is mystified to find all the lights in the building are off. *Maybe she isn't here yet?* she thinks. She shrugs to herself before pulling her own keys out and unlocking the door.

She opens it slowly and peers into the dark space. Something feels off.

But before she can process what she is feeling, the lights all click on and every one of her friends leap out of the shadows to proclaim, "Surprise!"

"Oh!" She starts and presses her hand to her chest before exhaling in relief and releasing a huge grin. "Guys! What's going on?"

She looks around to see her lobby decked out for a full-on house party. There are tables set up with plates and cups, as well as bowls and bowls of snacks and iced punch. Bottles of wine and beer are neatly arranged on the snack table as well, some out in the open and some nestled in ice buckets.

"Did you do all this?!" She looks around at them, and Sophia barrels toward her with open arms before pulling her into a tight grip.

"Yes! It was my idea," she exclaims with mock pride. She pulls away as Gisela bursts into giggles and looks into her eyes. "I'm just so happy you pulled us both out of that dead-end job. I didn't even realize how much that place was sucking the life out of me. It feels like... you saved us. And to think I almost didn't join you."

"Oh, Soph," Gisela coos. She grasps her friend's cheeks. "I couldn't have done any of this without you. Thank you for being here."

"And don't think I forgot..." Sophia trails off. "It's your 29th birthday!"

"Tomorrow," Gisela corrects.

"Oh, I know," Sophia says with a laugh. "But I figured—why not celebrate early!"

Gisela laughs alongside her. "Why not," she replies.

"Thirty is an amazing number, isn't it?" Monika calls. Her proclamation is met with sounds of agreement from most of the room. "Are you excited to be almost there?"

"Oh, yeah, sure," Gisela responds, stuttering slightly. *Excited?* she thinks. *Hardly.*

"Okay, enough mushy gushy feelings!" Monika interrupts. A loud *pop!* resounds as she busts open a bottle of champagne and its golden, fizzy liquid rains onto the floor. Thankfully, someone had the sense to lay a towel out first. "Let's *party*!!"

Sophia lets out a loud whoop and Gisela exchanges a look with Mia before cracking up with laughter.

There are pizzas laid out across the dining table, so everyone begins to divide and conquer, filling up plates and bowls with gooey, cheesy slices, chips, and candy. They clink together plastic cups of champagne and bottles of chilled beer.

As they all sit down to eat, they fill up the room with laughter and camaraderie. In a sense, each one of them has a leg in the game of L and L.

At some point, Sophia turns on the music and pulls Gisela and Mia both up to the dance floor. The three of them throw off their jackets and start flailing and jumping wildly about whatever clear space they can find.

Gisela's heart fills and the worries of her Oma and her now fast-approaching third decade of life begin to lift. She feels like a twenty-year-old again.

Jurgen cheers for them in the background, and amongst the chaos, Gisela spots Monika and Hans chatting in a corner.

Monika and Hans? she thinks. *Now that's a couple I never would have expected.* But it appears Monika has had a few glasses of wine at this point and is putting quite the charm on her brother's partner. Hans looks flustered and a little surprised, like he doesn't know what to do with the attention.

Klaus finishes the last of his beer before joining the ladies on their makeshift dance floor. He swoops in and grabs Sophia's hand before twirling her around in a graceful circle.

"Woah, Klaus! Moves!" Sophia shouts, her voice melting into bright, tinkling laughter as she follows his lead. He takes both of her hands and the two seem to meld together as one as they flounce and spin around each other. Gisela smiles to herself as she takes in the bashful flush across both of their cheeks.

It's been a long time coming, she muses.

She stops dancing and looks enough to look over at Jurgen, whose eyes are pointed fixedly on Mia.

And thank goodness we don't have to worry about that anymore.

Mia walks over to the snack bar and pours herself a glass of soda. Gisela watches as Jurgen slowly approaches from behind and seemingly whispers something over her shoulder.

Mia's head whips around and the second their eyes meet, Gisela can feel the tension and heat all the way across the room. Curious, she reaches out for their feelings. Both of them glow with deep hues of red and magenta. If nothing else, it's clear there's chemistry. She watches as they slip out of the lobby and towards the back hallway.

She raises a brow and smirks to herself. *Oh, to be a fly on the wall.* This thought brings her back to her meeting with Oma, and her chest pangs painfully. *I guess now I can be a fly on the wall. It would be a bit hard to explain my body slumping, unconscious on the ground in the middle of a party, though.*

She starts walking towards the dining table again, leaving Klaus and Sophia alone together on the dance floor. She slows as she approaches Monika and Hans, who seem very engaged in their current conversation.

Suddenly, in a room full of friends, she feels very much alone.

Alone and extremely single, and almost thirty, she thinks. Her stomach twists. She looks down at the beer in her hand. *Why did I even have to think about that right now? I should be having fun and focusing on my new business.*

Without thinking, she rushes out of the room and toward the hallway. *I can't really go to my office, it being made of glass and all.* She pauses at the door to Sophia's office instead, but as soon as she grabs the door handle, a soft moan drifts into the corridor.

Her face heats and her brows rise up instantaneously. *They make quick work of things, don't they?*

Feeling slightly frustrated, she passes by and walks into the break room. Thankfully, it is completely quiet.

She grabs a bottle of water from the fridge and starts sipping at it slowly. *I need to get out of my head.* She closes her eyes and allows herself to drift into a state of near meditation, emptying all of her thoughts and then replacing them with all her blossoming hopes for Leben and Lieben.

After a few minutes, this technique works, and she lets out a slow breath as her emotions settle.

Not long after, sharp footsteps come down the hallway, and hushed voices carry in front of them.

It sounds like Monika, Hans, and Jurgen are all talking, and from their tones, it sounds important.

"The visitors will be here soon," she hears Monika mutter, "we need to make sure they're ready. Is the project ready too?"

"Yes," Hans answers, "don't worry."

"I am worried," Monika snaps.

"Hey, hey, trust me, it's all working out smoothly. One of my old friends is actually already here. He—" Jurgen stops abruptly as he strides into the room and spots Gisela. "Oh! Birthday girl! I didn't know you were here."

"Hey there," Gisela replies slowly. She chugs a long gulp of water. "What's this about visitors? People you know?"

"Oh, yes!" Monika responds quickly. "We have a…" she trails off for a moment, her eyebrows scrunching together.

"A cousin," Jurgen fills in. He lets out an easy laugh before pinching Monika's arm. "Somebody's had a few drinks too many. Yes, our cousin Auri is in town right now. He came in from overseas. I think—"

"Let's not bore her with the details," Hans interrupts, voice deep and rumbling. "I think she has the right idea over there. Maybe let's grab some water for the others."

He opens the fridge and takes a few bottles out. Before anyone else, though, he steps closer to Monika and gently presses one into her hands. For a moment, their eyes meet, and something passes between them in silence.

There are too many things happening to keep track of, Gisela thinks. She clutches her head with frustration. *My head hurts.*

She spaces out as her friends continue their chatting, and soon enough, everyone else files into the small space. Still, Gisela can't seem to sort out one thought from another.

And what exactly is going on with those visitors they were talking about? she wonders. *I can't help but feel like they're all hiding something. And something tells me it's not another party.*

Chapter 10

Extravaganza and arrival

It's the morning of Leben and Lieben's grand opening, and Gisela is already up and ready to go at around six. She hasn't slept a wink since she woke up at three and doesn't know what to do to keep herself preoccupied.

She and Sophia spent hours sifting through applications for opening night and carefully curating a list of guests. Invitations have been sent out digitally, and all other preparations have been made. They are having an intimate gathering with catered hors d'oeuvre and drinks. Decorations are all in place and the menu has been finalized. There is quite literally nothing else for her to do.

So, she decides to take a walk.

She passes along the cool streets of Kreuzberg, shivering in the chill of dawn. The atmosphere is gray and quiet all around. The sun is just starting to rise over the water.

This was a smart decision, she thinks to herself. She lets out a deep, long breath and looks to the river as she walks. The cold invigorates her and she can feel her mind cycling through all the exciting prospects of her evening ahead.

Finally, the culmination of all our hard work. I cannot wait to see all those people there at the agency tonight.

As she's walking, she receives a text.

> Sophia: Am I the only one who couldn't sleep?! Good morning, partner; I hope you're ready for the best night of our lives!!

Gisela chuckles to herself and sends a quick text back with a few giddy emojis to go along with it.

Right after, she gets another text.

> Jurgen: Hey, Gisela, just wanted to let you know Sophia shared the guest list with me and Hans. I think she sent it to everyone. I'm pleased to see my cousin, Auri, is on there.

Gisela blinks and rubs her temple. *I do remember seeing that name. I completely forgot when he mentioned him the other night.* She continues reading.

> Jurgen: I also thought this was the best time to tell you some more people from out of the country came along with him, and I believe some of them are on your list too. I think this could be good; they're looking to learn more about the customs here and meet some people. I'm sure it'll be great for business. I look forward to tonight! See you then.

She types out a quick reply to him as well before slipping her phone back into her pocket.

What an interesting turn of events, she muses. *Foreigners. Perhaps I could teach them about Berlin. And the people here.* She felt her heartbeat pulse faster. The thrill of learning about new, interesting people excites her deeply. There is nothing quite like the subject of social customs and dating traditions to her.

She stops at a local coffee shop along her walk and picks up a hot latte to keep herself warm. As she returns to her all-too-familiar walking route, the sight of a less explored cobblestone street along the way compels her.

She stops at the street sign for a moment and looks down the street. *Why not?* she thinks. *Today is a day for newness.* With a smile and a slight skip in her step, she proceeds down the sidewalk.

Just as she turns, a short elderly woman emerges from a little store and flips the sign on the door over to read "Open."

She slows to approach her and reads the big, blue letters scrawled in cursive across the shop window. *It's a cat rescue!*

The woman at the door turns and looks at her with a warm smile. Her face lights up like a sunbeam and laugh lines crease invitingly across her cheeks.

"Good morning, young lady!" she greets. "Are you interested in coming inside?"

"I'd love to," Gisela breathes. The lady ushers her in and starts talking about how excited she is to have somebody come in first thing like this and how that almost never happens lately.

She listens politely with a few nods and a smile, but she feels immediately drawn towards an enclosure in the back where a few cats are lounging on cat trees and kittens are already running about playing.

"These are your cats?" she asks.

The old lady smiles brightly and nods. "Yes, my dear. Go ahead and step inside if you'd like."

Gisela has always had a special connection with animals, but she hasn't interacted with one in a long time. As she opens up the short gate and steps slowly into the cats' pen, she feels the corners of her eyes well with oncoming tears.

Not that I plan on becoming a lonely spinster surrounded by cats, she thinks, *but I would be lying to myself if I said having another living being around the house wouldn't be nice.*

As soon as she kneels down, a sleek tabby cat with a lovely, pale orange coat sidles up to her feet. He sits down in front of her and peers up with wide, green eyes.

She feels her heart tug inside her chest and reaches down to smooth her hand over his soft head. He lets out a high-pitched chirp and gives her a long blink before rubbing himself against her leg.

"Oh…" She murmurs.

"That's Oliver," the store owner says from behind the pony wall. "He's a real sweetheart. And he's probably been here the longest. He's about five years old now."

"I want him," Gisela replies quickly. She looks back at the lady with a sheepish smile. "May I adopt him?"

"Ooh, of course!" The lady claps her hands excitedly and grins. "My name is Brenda, by the way. Pleased to meet you, Ms?"

"Gisela," she tells her. She turns back to Oliver and smiles at him. Slowly, she reaches out to his mind—waves of unbridled affection and trust flow off of him. "Hello, little baby," she whispers. "I'm Gisela. It's time for you to have a home."

***

Gisela makes her way home right away to situate Oliver. She was able to buy all the necessities, like food, bowls, and of course, some treats at the very store she adopted him from. As she deposits him in her living room and watches him wander about, sniffing with curiosity at every little object, her own affection for this innocent creature swells and swells.

It isn't long before he's taken ownership of her house and settled in just fine. Although, it amuses Gisela to no end how he avoids the pet bed she bought for him and opts instead to lay in her armchair.

Naturally, she sends pictures of him to Sophia, Mia, and Monika.

She spends the time in between her morning escapade and getting ready for the grand opening watching Oliver, petting him, and talking to him. She uses her abilities on and off to reach out to him, and she notices whenever she does this, he seems to understand her words and tone on a deeper level.

This is almost more special than using it on a person, she thinks to herself.

During the late afternoon, she dresses herself in a navy-colored wool sweater and white trousers, pulls her honey-colored locks into a neat but elegant updo, and carefully applies her makeup. Oliver even follows her around as she flits between her dressing room and the bathroom.

Finally, she must leave home so she can meet Sophia and Mia at the agency before the event begins. Even though she was itching to get over there first thing in the morning, she now finds herself somewhat reluctant to leave Oliver behind when she does.

She gives him a few extra pats on his back and fills up his food and water bowls before leaving.

When she arrives at Leben and Lieben, Sophia and Mia are already inside, handling all the last-minute details and coordinating the servers they've hired for the event. Sophia is wearing a lovely tailored dress in a light pink shade, and Mia is wearing all black with a camera around her neck and a microphone already slung around her neck.

There are tablecloths on all of the tables and each one is laden with beautifully presented drinks and appetizers.

"Hey, ladies!" Gisela greets as she hustles into the building. "How's everything going?"

"Splendidly!" Mia responds with a warm smile. She gives Gisela a brief hug before gesturing about her. "All of this looks so lovely."

There are antique candelabras on the tables, already flickering with soft ambient light, and overflowing bouquets of freshly delivered flowers.

"Thank you," Gisela says, squeezing her arm.

Just as they finish chatting, the cameraman arrives to prepare for Mia's on-air coverage. And once six rolls around, people start lining up outside the front door.

Sophia walks up to Gisela, who is currently staring outside as more and more people accumulate. She can feel her heart thrumming wildly in her chest.

"You ready?" Sophia asks gently.

Gisela turns to her and gives her an uneasy smile. "I think so."

"We've got this," Sophia assures her. "Besides, we'll just be talking a little bit about our agency and then unleashing all the guests to eat, drink, and schmooze. Nothing huge."

"You're right." Gisela takes in a deep breath and smooths her hands down her trousers. "I'm ready when you are."

Sophia grins and gives her a quick squeeze around her shoulders. "Let's do it."

They walk to the front door together, open it, and Sophia calls out, "Everyone, come on in!" Meanwhile, Mia and the cameraman slip outside to begin shooting.

The guests stream inside, and Gisela gives them small smiles and polite greetings as she holds open the door. Several of them are unusually attractive, in an ethereal sort of way. She notes that some even appear related, sharing similarly sculpted faces, high cheekbones, pale, piercing eyes, and light hair.

Most of these guests are also wearing eye-catching jewelry, like bejeweled bracelets, dazzling pendants, and glimmering earrings that shift colors in a way she's never seen before.

I actually have, she realizes. *They look sort of similar to Jurgen and Monika's jewelry I always see them wear.*

And then she sees him.

The tall, devastatingly handsome man from ERA.

Her heart pounds like a roaring wave in her ears as time seems to slow down. She watches intently as he walks by; his long, white-blonde hair falls in a sleek sheath just past his shoulders and he is dressed in a perfectly tailored dress shirt unbuttoned at the top and a sleek black jacket.

When he passes Gisela, their eyes meet for a moment that feels like a breath of eternity.

His eyes are pale, pale blue, almost silver in appearance, and a smirk tilts the corner of his mouth up as he gives her a barely perceptible nod.

She doesn't realize she is holding her breath until he is gone. She shakes her head and begins breathing again, gasping quietly to herself for a second before she pulls herself together for the next guests.

She musters up a smile as they continue to file inside, but she can't quiet the turbulence still swirling in her brain.

Why does he affect me so much? she wonders. *What is it about him?*

As soon as the last guests shuffle in, Mia approaches Gisela and Sophia to ask them some quick questions about their agency. Gisela allows Sophia to take the lead, as her bubbling enthusiasm is perfect for this occasion. Once they are done, they walk inside.

Sophia reaches out to link arms with Gisela. "I'm nervous," she mumbles.

"Don't worry," Gisela says with a laugh, "you're doing great. Let's do this."

Sophia grins and they approach the front of the room. Gisela picks up a glass of champagne and delicately clinks a fork against its stem. Soon, everyone in the room is hushed, and they turn their faces toward the two of them.

"Ladies and gentlemen," she begins with a smile, "welcome to Leben and Lieben, Berlin's newest premier dating agency. Thank you so much for coming. We are so grateful to have this opportunity and to have you all here tonight. So let's make a toast."

Those guests carrying glasses lift them up.

"To Leben and Lieben," she shouts. "In more ways than one."

Each person echoes her toast and they all proceed to take a healthy sip from their glass. Gisela shares an excited look with Sophia. Finally, the mysterious man she encountered earlier is at the back of her mind, and all she can feel is bliss. Sophia gives her a nod even as she quietly takes a deep breath.

"Now," Gisela continues, "I'll let the lovely Sophia say a few words about our agency, and then you can continue the festivities."

***

About an hour later, Gisela and Sophia are conferring behind the snack bar about the progress of the event. They watch as their guests mill about, eat, and chat.

"Don't you think it's going amazingly?" Sophia enthuses. She looks at Gisela with a toothy grin and picks up a plate of crackers and meat from the charcuterie board. "Everyone seems to be having a great time."

"Yeah, I do," Gisela agrees with a slow nod. Her eyes, though, are primarily fixed on one individual. He is currently standing towards the back of the room, chatting with a group of individuals all bearing similarly regal features. It's then she realizes he fits in well with the odd guests she noticed earlier.

"Maybe some of the guests will spark some connections with each other here tonight," Sophia continues. She trails off when she realizes Gisela isn't engaged and follows her line of sight. "Oh! Have you met Jurgen and Monika's cousin, Auri? He's standing over there with that… strange group of people. Actually, I wonder if those are the other foreigners Jurgen talked about. They all seem to look alike and dress the same."

"Auri?" Gisela asks, tearing her gaze away to look at Sophia. She furrows her brow. "Wait, *that* man is Jurgen and Monika's cousin?" She glances back at him. "Oh."

"Yeah…" Sophia replies. She looks at Gisela with a soft smirk. "You seem oddly interested in him. Maybe you should talk."

"Oh, I don't know," Gisela stammers. She coughs and looks down into her drink. "You think those are the foreigners?" She looks back up at the people gathered around Auri. "What do you think of them? They've all been acting kind of aloof, and I get this sort of spiritual vibe when I talk to them."

"Yeah, I got the same thing," Sophia answers. She raises an eyebrow before taking a bite of her snack. "Honestly, I don't know how I feel about them. They seem kind of weird. I can see why they're all single, though."

"What do you mean?" Gisela asks.

"I can't explain it," Sophia sighs. "There's just something… off-putting about them. They're somehow too intense and too distant at the same time. You know," she snaps her fingers and grins. "They kind of remind me of Jurgen. Oh, I'm so glad he's been panting after Mia lately."

"Me too," Gisela laughs. "Personally, I'm rooting for you and Klaus."

Sophia flushes and smiles to herself. "Actually, I was going to tell you something, but I haven't had the chance."

Gisela gapes and turns to face her. She grabs her arm with one hand. "Is that what I think?" she breathes. "Did Klaus finally ask you on a date?"

Sophia nods and shyly grins.

"Oh. My. Gosh!" Gisela squeals. "I am so happy for you! You need to tell me all about it when it's over. Where are you going?"

Sophia shrugs. "It's a surprise. I never took Klaus for the spontaneous or adventurous type."

"Me either," Gisela admits, "but that man is definitely full of surprises."

"Yeah, but it took him long enough," Sophia jokes.

Gisela laughs before loosening her grip on Sophia's arm and pulling her close. She rests her head against Sophia's shoulder and looks out at the crowd.

Gisela finds her eyes drawn once more to Auri, as much as she wants to ignore him. *If only he would look at me,* she thinks.

Not a moment later, those intense blue eyes shift in her direction, and their gazes connect.

She feels her breath hitch in her throat, and embarrassment burns her cheeks, but she can't look away.

His eyes move down her figure, so fast and imperceptible she isn't sure she saw it right. But when he locks eyes with her again, he flashes that same small smirk from before, and she knows she did.

Okay, he can look away now, she thinks, *because I don't think I can.*

And just like that, he looks away.

Did I just… do that? She wonders. She frowns to herself. *There's no way… right?*

She shakes those thoughts away from her mind and takes in a long, deep breath. *I don't have time to worry about some strange man. Look at all this in front of me.* She looks down at Sophia, who is still watching the party before them with awe.

Gisela tries to put her focus away from Auri and the strange foreigners and instead concentrate on the beautiful masterpiece unfolding before them. Their own work of art is finally coming to fruition.

Chapter 11

Dream client or a shadow of

Doubt

The next couple of weeks fly by almost seamlessly for Leben and Lieben. Each day Gisela sits down in her office to start her work day, she can hardly believe her life now is even real.

She and Sophia have been positively flooded with work, though; trying to keep up with the already insane demand for their business has kept them on their toes every minute of the day.

Of course, there's been a bit of trial and error for them as well. As it's their first time actually using the system they built with Jurgen and Hans, they have to work out some kinks along the way.

Gisela has also had her hands full, evaluating every customer's profile and tailoring match recommendations. Even though it's been challenging, it's also the most fulfilling work she's done in her entire life. She could choose to fully automate the systems and let her computer do most of the work, but she prides herself on the personal touches she brings to the table.

And so far, it's proven immeasurably successful.

It takes time to set clients up with other clients, build lists for them, and watch their escapades play out, so only a handful have actually gone on dates with their matches. And yet, each one has left glowing reviews on Leben and Lieben's website and a couple have even thanked her personally.

She's also been experimenting with something she suspects to be another spiritual ability of hers. It seems like a form of manifestation, and it started the night she wanted Auri to look at her.

Curious about the way his actions seemed to mirror her thoughts, she started thinking little things into fruition, like Sophia brewing coffee for them without asking or their takeout deliveries being given to them for free.

So far, each time has worked out.

She decides to table it for now and ask Bast about it the next time they meet. She's not sure if the idea excites or terrifies her.

Gisela sits down in her office the Monday morning of Leben and Lieben's third week of business with a reusable thermos brimming with iced coffee and her tried and true tote bag carrying just as many notebooks and writing utensils as it always has.

Sophia is already there, and she walks by Gisela's office with a broad smile and a grin before ducking back down the hallway.

I can't believe I'm working at my own company with my best friend, Gisela thinks to herself. She finds herself repeating this sentiment over and over again in her head nearly every day.

From having no more Katherine looming over her at all hours, working on something meaningful to her, producing tangible results every day with Sophia, to mid-day chats in their personalized break room and a building filled with music and laughter whenever they want, Gisela couldn't ask for a better workplace.

She's starting up her PC for the day and writing in her planner when she hears a firm knock at her office door.

When she looks up, her heart stills in her chest.

"Come in," she calls, but she struggles to keep her voice even.

Oh my god. It's him. Auri.

Auri opens the glass door and gives her a slow, swoon-worthy smile. His long, pale hair is held back in a half-up half-down style that makes him look like an elven prince. She can't wrap her head around the ethereal beauty of this man.

"Hello, Ms. Gisela. I've been told by my cousins, Monika and Jurgen, that you are the woman to talk to around here," he begins. "I'd like to introduce myself. I'm Auri."

She hastily stands up and curses internally when her chair wobbles against her legs with the force. "Hello, Auri," she responds. She smooths her hands over her navy blue trousers and musters a small smile. "That depends on what you'd like to talk about, but yes, I suppose I probably would be the woman you're seeking." Her face heats when she realizes the subtle implications of her words.

He raises an eyebrow as a dreadfully attractive smirk replaces his smile. He walks up to her desk and holds out his hand.

"Pleasure to meet you," he murmurs.

She glances down at his outstretched hand. She could swear he must hear her heart drumming nervously against her chest.

Take his hand, Gisela, she scolds herself.

She thrusts out her own hand and tucks a loose hair behind her ear with the other. He gently takes her hand in his and gives it a firm shake.

For some reason, the touch of his skin against hers sets sparks racing down her stomach and spine. She takes in a short breath and looks away from his searing eye contact.

"Same to you," she replies, "I think."

Gisela! Why did you add that? She winces at her choice of words and looks back up at him with pleading eyes.

He lets out a soft chuckle.

"No worries," he assures her. He gestures to the chair on his side of her desk as their hands fall apart. "Shall we sit?"

"Yes," she says quickly. She sits down in her own chair as he does in his. "I'm sorry for my awkwardness; you are just stunningly—" She cuts herself off as a rush of burgundy floods her cheeks. *Shut up, shut up, shut up!*

"Stunningly…?" He queries. There is laughter dancing in his eyes.

"I may as well finish it," she groans. She looks away before returning his stare with a shy smile. "I was going to say stunningly handsome," she admits.

"Thank you," he answers. His voice is deep and rumbling, with a soothing and earnest quality that begins to set her at ease. "I don't often receive compliments from a woman as gorgeous as you. I appreciate your boldness."

Her throat clenches and her eyes go wide as the room seems to freeze. She stares at him blankly.

"Please tell me you do realize how attractive *you* are," he continues, and part of her wishes he would stop even as butterflies flutter pleasantly in her stomach. Embarrassment and excitement mingle as one within her.

"I—I don't know," she says, her voice coming out more aggressive than she intended. She takes a deep breath before adjusting in her seat. She faces his stare once again. "I know I'm not *unattractive*."

"Good," he replies. The smirk returns. "I was afraid for a moment I'd have to point you to a mirror and explain every single part of your face to you."

"Oh," she breathes.

A silence, thick with anticipation and something even Gisela couldn't discern, fills the space around them.

"Anyway," she continues, breaking the tension with forced finality. "May I ask what you're coming here for… Mr. Auri?"

"I actually have a business proposition for you," he answers. He leans towards her, and she can smell the faintest whiffs of mint and lemon on his breath. "I know you know some of the guests at your grand opening were foreigners like me… there are many others, as well. Most of them are unfamiliar with this place's customs, especially when it comes to love." He seems to pause on the last word, and his eyes briefly dart to her lips.

She freezes and her mouth dries up.

"Even aside from dating," he goes on, "I know participating in something like Leben and Lieben could give them valuable experience interacting with the locals here. Something I think they desperately need. You could probably tell they aren't the most… charismatic bunch."

"They did seem a little off," she admits. "Sorry," she quickly adds, "I don't mean to be rude."

He laughs loudly. "No, no, please, continue to be honest. I appreciate it." His eyes sparkle and he leans back in his chair. "Anyway, I'd like to sponsor these people to allow them a place in your agency so they can begin assimilating into your lovely culture. I am prepared to pay premium prices… although, we would need to figure out a way to process my currency for now; I haven't yet had anything converted into euros."

"Honestly, this sounds like an amazing opportunity," Gisela answers. She scratches her chin slowly. *And I certainly wouldn't mind seeing him on a day-to-day basis,* she muses. "I'd be interested in helping them to integrate into our society. I love studying people and studying the culture around dating and relationships. And I'm sure we could figure out a way to process your payment. Since it's such a large group, I won't charge any extra for me to convert it for you."

"Fantastic," he says. His smirk builds into a grin, and somehow as his face lights up, she finds him even more attractive. "I don't have my payment on hand, but I will bring it by later, along with all the specifics for this group. In the meantime, will you draft up a contract for us?"

"Yes, I will," she says with a nod.

They both stand and she finds herself wishing this impromptu meeting would last just a little bit longer.

He pauses before leaving and stares at her with something indeterminable in his gaze. Suddenly, he reaches out a hand and brushes it through a loose honey-colored lock hanging beside her cheek.

She sucks in a breath and stares at him with big, hopeful eyes.

He smiles, this time softly, and lets his hand slowly fall away.

"It's been wonderful meeting you, Gisela." She can hardly bear the sound of her name on his tongue, and she offers a smile in return.

"Same for you, Auri." He gives her a nod before turning and exiting the room. She watches him walk through the lobby and out the front door before she finally collapses back into her seat.

"Oh my god," she breathes. She can finally feel her heartbeat slowing in her chest. She gulps and looks down at the planner in front of her. "How does he do that?" She blinks before picking her pen back up and bringing it to the page. "I guess I have a lot more to plan out now," she mumbles.

***

Auri returns later that afternoon to finalize the payments and sign all the necessary paperwork. He also provides Gisela with a folder full of all the needed information for her new clients; she isn't sure what she was expecting but it wasn't for him to be this prepared so quickly.

After he leaves, she looks through the folder and realizes immediately she is going to have her work cut out for her. She flips through the pages, a mixture of alarm and fascination growing rapidly in her gut. *There are at least twenty-odd pages in here,* she thinks. *That's twenty-something new clients to upload into the system and coach through the dating customs here.*

She looks out of her office and towards the hallway absent-mindedly. *Sophia will want to hear about this,* she muses, *and my brain could use a break right now.* She stands up and hurries to the break room.

Unsurprisingly, Sophia is already there, sipping her third cup of coffee for the day.

"Can your nerves handle that much caffeine?" Gisela teases.

Sophia looks up from her book with a smile. "You know, I find that ever since leaving that god-awful workplace, my nerves are quite settled, thank you very much."

"Whatcha reading?" Gisela asks. She slides into the seat opposite Sophia at her table.

"Oh, just this new romance novel from a local author," Sophia replies. She bookmarks her spot at the beginning of a chapter and closes it. She looks up at Gisela with a raised eyebrow. "Something on your mind?"

"Well…" Gisela leans forward conspiratorially. "I may have just landed our first really big client."

"Really? Who?" Sophia presses. Her brown eyes go wide.

"Actually, it's Monika and Jurgen's cousin," Gisela answers. She leans back in her seat and reveals a huge grin. "Auri."

"I did see him in your office earlier," Sophia admits. She purses her lips. "Not that I was prying, of course. So wait, what kind of deal? Does it have anything to do with those strange people at the grand opening?"

"I think so," Gisela answers with a nod. She scratches her shoulder and gives her a small shrug. "He says they need help acclimating to our culture and the dating customs here. He's willing to pay extra for me to coach them too."

"How surprising," Sophia jokes. Gisela gives her an arch look. "Well, it's just… they don't give me the best vibe, to be honest." Sophia lets out a slow sigh. "I don't mean to rain on your parade. But when I was watching you with Auri in there, I just kept getting this weird feeling."

"Why a weird feeling?" Gisela asks. She can feel her stomach drop in disappointment. *The first man I'm interested in, and already my best friend doesn't like him.*

"That's the thing," Sophia responds. She looks down at her coffee. "I don't know. So I didn't wanna say anything. But since we're going into business with him… just be careful, okay? I hope my intuition is wrong, but…"

"I know," Gisela soothes. She rests her hand on Sophia's and her friend gives her a grateful smile. "I know you're just looking out for me. And intuition shouldn't be ignored. I'll watch out, okay? I'll try to keep things strictly professional."

Sophia smiles sadly and takes another sip of her drink. "You like him, don't you?"

Gisela feels her cheeks heat up like a flame. "I mean, he's attractive," she mumbles, "but I don't really know him yet. But I guess I'd be lying if I said I don't want a relationship. I'm kind of tired of not having somebody."

"Oh, sweetie, I'm sorry." Sophia squeezes her hand. "Don't rule him out just yet. We'll get to see his character while we're working with him, I'm sure. And I promise I'll keep my mind open."

"Thanks," Gisela replies. She lets out a relaxed breath. "I'm excited about this, actually. I guess I better get back to my office and start putting in their information."

"How many clients are there, exactly?" Sophia queries.

Gisela shoots her a serious look. "At least twenty-four," she replies.

"Oh, gosh, wow." Sophia blinks and looks at her with amusement in her eyes. "I guess I should return to my office too. Email me the information about payments and I'll take care of logging everything into the system."

"Will do." Gisela smiles as they both stand up and return to their spaces.

⁎

Gisela spends the rest of her workday plugging in information on each client. It turns out there are twenty-seven of them in total, which has her thinking all the way home about how she can most effectively teach them about the dating customs of Berlin.

Finally, during her nighttime routine, she realizes a group of this volume is going to need more personal attention. So she logs in to L and L's program on her personal computer and makes plans for an introductory course before sending digital invitations out to all of the foreigners.

Despite how late it is, most of them RSVP almost immediately. The next day, when she looks over all of the responses, she sees they all answered yes.

When the evening of the introductory course arrives the following Wednesday, just after business hours end, Gisela finds herself opening the locked door and greeting all twenty-seven of them.

At the end of the line is Auri, and he approaches her with a dangerously sly smirk as the others file inside.

He is dressed in a knit, navy blue sweater that fits his tall, slender figure to perfection and tailored black trousers.

He may have just gotten here, but his style is impeccable, Gisela muses.

"Are you ready for tonight, Gisela?" he asks. She feels goosebumps rise along her skin when he says her name, and she manages to force a small smile even as her nerves explode beneath her skin.

"Your presence is making me a bit unsure," she admits without thinking.

He laughs and shakes his head. "I like the honesty." He moves closer until she can smell the cognac-scented cologne on his clothes.

She gulps and looks into his eyes. They narrow, and for a second, she feels as if he can read into her very soul. She feels something tug at her head as if someone is pulling her hair. But when she lifts her hand, nothing is there.

Then the feeling passes, and he leans away again. He gestures inside and takes hold of the door. "After you," he continues. His voice is low and silky, and she finds herself rubbing her arms even though she isn't cold.

She nods and ducks inside in a rush to hide the heat creeping across her face. She finds her clients waiting in the lobby, chatting and mingling quietly. She takes a moment to survey the room.

They don't seem ill-tempered or ill-mannered, at least for now. I can't see them being too hard to work with. They'll surely be an interesting case study, to say the least.

Many of them are wearing bold, flashy jewelry like they were at the grand opening. Although, when she looks at Auri, she notices she doesn't notice anything on his person except a thin gold band around his wrist. When he moves his arm, though, a thousand colors seem to sparkle in the light. It's as if the gold links are inlaid with a dazzling and dark rainbow of crystals.

She walks to the front of the room and calls for their attention. The soft noise quickly dies down as they turn to face her. Auri joins her but stands a few feet behind her. She can feel his focused stare on the back of her neck, and it sends goosebumps down her spine.

"I'm so glad all of you are here today," she says with a small smile. She looks around at all the curiously watchful eyes peering back at her. "I'm going to cut right to the point. Since you are such a large group, and Leben and Lieben isn't yet used to working with such a high volume of clients or completing the scope of coaching you require, I'm going to take you all through weekly lessons until I feel you are comfortable with the dating customs of our city."

She takes a deep breath and glances back at Auri. He gives her an encouraging nod and a smirk she tries to ignore.

She turns back around and continues, "Today, I figured we would just take some time to run an introductory meeting. I'll get to know all of you some more and the scope of your knowledge. At the end of the night, we can discuss possible curriculum as well as when and what your first official lesson will entail."

A man in the group with shoulder-length black hair speaks up. "When will we start meeting one on one with our matches?" he asks.

There is something striking and intriguing about his appearance. His face is sharp and masculine, and there is a boldness in his dark eyes, which could either be off-putting or appealing.

"I don't have a time frame yet for our lessons," Gisela answers, "but tonight, I will be able to assess the scope of your current knowledge and we can go from there. But I'd like to integrate you better into our culture so when you do start meeting your matches, they will be much more successful."

She answers a few more questions after this, most of them from the same man, who later reveals his name is Lucien. Then the night proceeds, and she discovers this group of people, while mostly easygoing, needs a lot of preparation before entering the dating world.

This is going to take weeks, maybe even a few months, she thinks to herself. At the end of the night, she asks them to meet her back at the agency in a week's time to begin their lessons. As she watches them all leave, a ball of adrenaline starts building in her gut. She can't deny this is the most excited she's ever been.

Chapter 12

Educating and assimilating begins

A few weeks pass with ease; Gisela spends her first lessons with the foreigners teaching them inside the agency about Berlin and the dating world. She talks about topics such as first introductions, body language, being open and genuine, conversation, listening, and even chemistry.

They seem to catch on relatively quickly, and each one is equally as eager every week to get out there and start seeing people.

Oddly enough, most of them are men, although there are a handful of women too. Sometimes she wonders why none of the women are interested in the men in their group.

Maybe they're looking for something different, she muses one night after she splits everyone up into mock "dates" to watch their conversational skills with each other in action.

Sophia hasn't been present for any of the lessons yet, but she decided to stay late to observe this one. She watches them now beside Gisela with an air of uncertainty hanging about her.

"Are you okay?" Gisela asks her. Sophia's brow is currently creased with worry.

"Yeah, it's just," she pauses and sighs. "I ran into one of the guys in the hallway earlier. He was looking for the bathroom. And the way he looked at me... I don't know how to describe it. It's like he scanned me. And then I guess he didn't see anything he was looking for because he just pushed past me without another word."

"That's weird." Gisela fingers her chin thoughtfully. "Did you catch his name? I may just have to talk to them about... manners. And being considerate of people even when they aren't interested in them."

"No, I didn't," Sophia responds. "And yeah, I'll say." She scoffs and examines her nails. "I'm telling you, Gisela, these guys give me the creeps. Even the women seem a little off. They're all really beautiful too. It's like they're arrogant or something and think they're above everyone."

"Maybe they are," Gisela says with a shrug. "I'll try to correct that." She turns to look at Sophia. "But Sophia, I swear, Auri is… different. He's never come across as creepy or weird to me."

"I'm glad to hear it," an amused voice purrs from behind her.

Gisela's cheeks burn hot immediately and she watches the laughter dance in Sophia's amber eyes.

She whips around to face none other than the man in question himself. "Auri!" She exclaims. "I—" She breaks off and looks away.

"It's okay," he eases. "I actually wanted to ask you if you would maybe take me through one of these mock dates yourself. I know I'm not technically a client right now, but I'd like to practice some of these techniques, too, if that's okay."

"Oh!" Gisela gulps a growing lump down her throat and uses all her willpower to ignore the searing look Sophia is giving her. "Sure," she answers. "I'd love to… show you that. A mock date, of course."

Auri smirks and nods before holding out his hand. "Maybe you'd take me somewhere a little more… quiet to practice? And perhaps Ms. Sophia wouldn't mind watching them out here for us?" He looks at her friend with a cocked brow.

Sophia grins and shrugs before saying, "Sure, I could do that. You kids have fun." She waggles her brows at Gisela unabashedly, serving only to flush her cheeks with more heat.

"Thank you," Auri replies.

Gisela gently places her hand in his. "We could sit in the breakroom," she says.

"Very romantic," he teases.

She rolls her eyes before releasing a relieved laugh. *Calm down and focus, Gisela,* she tells herself, *or you'll never get through this. Besides, I'm sure he doesn't bite.*

As they walk through the hallway, she feels him rub a finger softly against her wrist and she halts. He pulls her close to his chest and she swears her heartbeat stops completely.

"I'll only bite if the situation calls for it," he whispers.

Oh. She gasps quietly and sucks in a deep breath. *It's like he read my mind. Except, he couldn't possibly, right?*

She turns around and looks into his pale eyes. He arches a brow, and it feels like a challenge. Except she has no idea how to accept.

"Perhaps your first lesson," she breathes, "should be on forwardness and palatability."

"Oh, yes?" he teases. He steps closer and leans in until their noses almost touch. "What about it do I need to learn?"

"You come on way too strong," she states, keeping her voice calm even though her head is pounding and her mind is foggy with heat. "You need to learn some subtlety." With this, she turns back around and drags him into the breakroom.

His laughter echoes in the space around them, and the tightness in her chest releases. No matter how on edge she feels when he speaks, there is something warmly familiar and comforting about the sound of his laugh. She can't quite place it.

Through their mock date conversation, Gisela finds herself unsure of why he asked her to do it in the first place. *He's much more accustomed to the culture and far more well-mannered than any of the other foreigners. Maybe it's Jurgen and Monika's influence?* she wonders. He listens attentively and offers genuine responses. In every way, he's the perfect suitor.

So why did he want to bring me here? A thrill of hope flickers in her chest at all the vague possibilities running around her mind.

***

The next week, on the day before the group's next lesson, Gisela is planning their first outing when Monika comes into the agency.

"How can I help?" she asks as her friend opens the door to her office and darts right in.

She raises an eyebrow and smiles with amusement at the fact she didn't even feel the need to knock.

"Yes," Monika answers, sounding breathless. "I'm on my break, so I don't have much time. I just wanted to ask you if I could shadow you tomorrow?"

"Shadow... me?" Gisela asks, furrowing her brow. "What do you mean?"

"Oh, you know, follow you around and see what you do during the day. I guess I'm just curious about the business and I want to learn more about your day-to-day so I can better know how to market for you." She pauses, and something seems to hold her tongue for a moment. "And... I was hoping I could sit in on your lesson with Auri and the others."

"Oh, sure," Gisela responds. "I don't see why not. But you do know you could've just called, right?"

Monika grins. "I was out on a light power walk anyway. Okay, thank you, bye!" She rushes out of her office just as fast as she came in.

Gisela blinks and rubs her forehead. "Okay..." she mutters. "Odd." She shrugs to herself and returns to her planning. She's extremely excited for this outing, as she will be taking the foreigners out about town. They won't be interacting with other customers yet, but she will teach them in action about friendly exchanges with other strangers, like store owners, stall vendors, and even random people in the street.

She wants to encourage them out of their comfort zone and get them more familiar with Kreuzberg while she's at it. *I'm sure they'll be falling in love with the city before they fall in love with anyone else,* she muses. *What's not to love about this place?*

The next day, Monika hangs out around Leben and Lieben. Since much of the work is done on computers, she flits between Gisela and Sophia's offices.

Gisela brings her through their patented matchmaking program and shows her a glimpse of her personal process for matchmaking. Monika even gets to meet a couple of clients who drop in to receive Gisela's reports and learn about their potential matches.

It thankfully turns out to be one of their most productive and eventful days, and the hours fly by. Monika proves to be useful, too; she goes on coffee and lunch runs for them and even offers to sort through some paperwork. It's hard not to appreciate her direct, task-oriented personality on days like this.

When the workday ends and the foreigners arrive for their outing, Monika falls back and watches with intense interest. Gisela had never seen her quite so focused.

The foreigners do wonderfully, for the most part. Many are still a bit awkward in talking with the strangers running stalls outside, but Gisela has worked with them on treating people who aren't romantic interests with care.

As she watches a few of them order and receive coffee from a small stall on the same bridge she and Mia love to run on, she finds herself swelling with pride as they smile at the barista and thank him for their drinks. One even slips a tip into his glass jar, and she lets out a long breath.

"Things seem to be coming along nicely," Monika remarks, "do you think you'll set them up on their first dates soon?"

"Yes, actually," Gisela confirms, "they've been doing much better. And today has given me hope. I think for our next meeting, I'm going to organize something with the other customers and test the waters."

"I think that's a great idea," Monika agrees quickly. Her eyes sparkle with excitement.

Gisela eyes her curiously. "Got your eye on somebody here?" she teases.

"Oh! No, no," Monika lets out a breezy laugh. "It's just nice to see the people from my home… country get along so well here. Jurgen and I have been anticipating it. And, of course, it's amazing for Leben and Lieben."

Gisela nods and turns back to watch as Auri guides someone through ordering a drink. She can't help but think back to their last interaction when he asked her to walk him through a mock date like the others. Her skin flushes lightly, and butterflies awaken in her stomach. *Don't be like a teenage girl,* she scolds herself, *just calm down.*

"I think I'm going to talk with some of them," Monika announces. She flounces off toward a small cluster of the foreigners, including the man named Lucien.

Gisela can just barely hear the subject of conversation, but what she does pick up on leaves her confounded. She catches a few words like "reporting the progress," "Collective," and "Oracle." It's almost as if they're speaking in code… or just talking about something she knows nothing about.

As she stands there, she focuses her mind on the group, reaching out for even a sliver of emotion or thought.

She bounces between each one, including Monika, but it's as if some invisible wall is bouncing her away. She flinches and grabs the side of her head as a sharp pang slams into it.

"Okay, geez, I get the hint," she mumbles. She sighs and tries to bury the disappointment burrowing in her gut. *Is something wrong with my powers?* she wonders. *I need to call my Oma.*

Chapter 13

Vulnerability and tension

At the end of their lesson, Gisela announces to the group she is going to be integrating them with the rest of her clients next. She truly feels they are almost ready for actual matches and one-on-one dates.

This news seems to go over well with them all, especially Monika and Auri. As Gisela watches them react, she wonders about the strange sense of familiar camaraderie between them.

I know they're cousins, she muses, *but they haven't seen each other in years and years.*

She doesn't bother bringing them back to the agency after the outing since none of them left anything there, and she watches from the sidelines after dismissing them as they slowly disperse and head in different directions toward home. Auri and Monika hang back to chat, though, and once the rest of the clients have left, they drift over to her side.

"I'm going to call it a night," Monika announces. Something strange glints in her eyes as she glances between Gisela and Auri. "You two have a… good night."

Gisela blinks rapidly and crooks her head. Normally her friend doesn't speak so vaguely; she's always shared a similar way of bluntness and candor with her that brought them that much closer. She can't help but wonder what would cause Monika to speak so cryptically.

"Goodnight, Monika," she replies with a smile. Auri simply nods and gives the brunette a small wave. In just a few moments, she is striding quickly away from them, her cadence confident and almost jovial.

Gisela looks towards Auri, who is eyeing her with curiosity and something else she can't quite define. She realizes they're alone now, and she can feel her breath instinctively hitch in her throat. Her heart catches up a second later, already drumming faster and faster with the passing silence.

Time seems to still as she looks into his bright eyes. They reflect in the growing moonlight and his mouth slowly turns into a smirk.

"Gisela, my Liebling," he says, and all the breath in her body whooshes out of her chest.

He's never called me that before, she thinks. She tightens her fingers on the strap of her purse and turns eagerly to give him her attention. For once, she's at a loss for words.

"I have a question for you," he continues, voice slow and deliberate. He steps closer to her and leans in. At this point, she can hardly hear him speak above the roaring in her own chest.

His face drifts near hers, and that startling stare focuses for a hazy moment on her lips before flitting back up to her eyes.

"Would you accompany me on a date?" he murmurs.

"Oh!" she exclaims softly. She coughs lightly to try and clear the lump in her throat. "Obviously," she blurts. A flush of color rushes to her cheeks. "I mean, yes, sure I would."

He nods and backs away with a grin. "As a favor, of course. I simply want to hone my skills in a… real-life setting. I know I'm not technically a client, but… I have been considering becoming one."

Just like that, her stomach drops. "Oh, I see," she responds. She tries to keep the disappointment out of her tone, but it's hard to keep her emotion from betraying her. "Well, I suppose I could spare an hour or two to, uhm… help you out."

He nods and lets out a long breath. He reaches out his arm and smiles down at her softly. "Would you take my arm?" he asks. "I have a place scoped out for us already."

She gives him a tight smile back and takes his arm. She tries to ignore the way it feels to walk so close as they proceed down the street. *Surely he must know what he's doing here,* she thinks. Frustration wells in her gut and tightens her chest like a fist. *Is he just trying to mess with me?*

Disappointment pokes like a dagger as she struggles to push away her feelings of inadequacy.

All this time, all my years alive, and still nobody has shown this much interest in me. And yet, it isn't even real. When will it be my turn? How long do I have to wait?

They make it to a small, intimate restaurant with outdoor seating and he leads her to a small table tucked into a corner. There is a vase of fresh flowers and a few small candles across its surface.

He pulls her chair out like a true gentleman, just as she's taught the others to do, and they settle in. The mood is entirely romantic and endearing, but she can't untangle the webs of uncertainty from her mind.

As the so-called date progresses, though, it gets harder and harder to acknowledge those unpleasant strings. They fall into easy conversation, and every time his eyes meet hers or their legs brush together under the table, her breath hitches in an instant.

It's undeniable, and even though his actions towards her have been strange, she knows there is no way he could deny the attraction between them.

A heat glows between them brighter than the candles on their table.

At the end of dinner, he reaches for their check at the same time she does, so their hands barely touch.

She freezes and gives him a shy smile.

He smiles back and runs his fingers tenderly over her knuckles before resting his hand gently on her own.

This simple contact is enough to send a jolt of warmth across her whole body, and she knows with certainty now this chemistry is real.

But is he acting this way because he cares or because he's trying to succeed on this mock date?

His smirk falters for a moment, though, when their hands meet. It's barely perceptible, but she notices a slight intake of air, and his eyes grow dark.

She trembles. The air around them stills.

And then, as fast as the moment came, it leaves. He gulps and plasters on a smile once again before darting his touch away and clicking his tongue.

"Ah, ah, ah," he chides, "dinner is on me tonight. I'm trying to be a gentleman here." He arches a brow at her and she shakes her head with a nervous laugh. She tears her gaze away, trying to calm her rushing heartbeat.

She looks back up at him. "It seems to come pretty naturally for you," she comments.

His eyes darken once more for barely an instant. "Trust me," he says, voice as low as a growl, "I am definitely not a gentleman in most situations."

Oh, heavens, she muses. Her knees knock together and she squirms uncomfortably in her seat. *What is wrong with me, to let this man affect me so much when he's barely broken a sweat over me?*

They finish the date in relative quiet, and he walks her back to her neighborhood. As they find themselves stopping a couple of blocks away from her house, she slowly comes to a stop. She looks up at him and smiles, but thoughts are still whirring like a hurricane in her mind.

"So," he says slowly, "how did I do?"

"Auri…" she pauses. She only barely registers his question because her own head is fuzzy from feelings and thoughts bursting and begging to be let out. She isn't normally able to hold them in for so long, but this thing between them has felt so unsure and high-stakes she couldn't bring herself to before.

But not anymore.

It still feels uncertain, maybe even more so, which is exactly why she must confront him with everything now.

"Auri, I like you," she exclaims. When she realizes how loud she is, drawing a confused glance from a couple walking on the other side of the road, she clears her throat and quiets herself. "I don't know what it is," she continues, "but I'm very attracted to you. And I think you're attracted to me too."

He levels her with an arch look, but she keeps going.

"I know this date wasn't... real. However, I want to go on another one with you. A real one." She pauses and looks away. "So there. I've said all I need to say. And you did great, by the way. Almost perfect."

He stands there in silence for a few seconds, and she forces her eyes back up to his own. They are swirling with something she can't discern, something completely foreign. He tucks his hands in his pant pockets and lets out a low sigh.

When she reaches out with her mind to get a glimpse of those unreadable feelings, she gets nothing back at all. There isn't a wall quite like Monika's, but it almost feels as if a thick curtain has been thrown over Auri's mind and she just can't see through.

"I need to go," he finally answers. "I like you a lot, Gisela, but I don't think I see pursuing a relationship together. Have a goodnight. Goodbye."

She gapes and stares as he turns on his heel and walks away. His steps are long and his stride is completely unbothered.

I can't tell if he's insufferable... or insufferably appealing. She groans aloud and resigns herself to head back home.

Chapter 14

OMG! More weird happenings

For Gisela's clients' first introduction to the rest of L and L's membership base, she's arranged a casual speed dating session for them, hosted by a local restaurant that's agreed to privatize a section of their space for them.

She spends just about the whole week leading up to it planning, sending out invitations to a select number of her clients, and making arrangements. Normally it would only take her a day or two to get everything in order, but her mind is so distracted by her night with Auri she can hardly think straight throughout the workday.

Auri doesn't come into the agency all week either, and she isn't sure if she's relieved or concerned. Some small part of her still is a little upset.

One afternoon at the office, she decides to call her Oma. She intends to confide in her about her issues with Auri, but when she actually answers the phone, Gisela balks. Instead, she talks about her problems reading the minds of Monika and the foreigners.

Bast isn't much help, though, and she remains curt and passive during their whopping eight-minute call.

"You just need to keep practicing," she tells her. "It's important to keep your abilities in… prime shape."

"Why do I even need to do that?" Gisela snaps. "Sometimes these so-called gifts feel more like a burden." Her stomach turns. She isn't usually so honest with Oma about her feelings, but there's no point dwelling on it once the words are out.

Instead of the annoyance or anger she expects, Bast simply lets out a long sigh. Disappointment coats her tone as she responds with a simple, "You will see, eventually." Somehow, this response is even worse.

"There is something else," she admits after a moment of silence. Part of her wants to keep Bast on the phone, even though the air between them is still tense after their last altercation. "Lately, I've been… sort of manifesting things happening. I'll think of something, like someone looking at me or coming over or bringing me something, and it will happen. Do you know what to make of that?"

"Oh." Bast pauses, but her tone has done a complete 180. Hope sparks in Gisela's chest like a dim match. "Yes, very good," she replies. *She sounds almost… excited,* Gisela muses. "Keep doing that," she adds, "and update me on our next meeting. I have to go now. Goodbye."

Before Gisela can even get a word in edgewise, her Oma hangs up. She twists her mouth in a frown and sets her cell phone down on her desk.

***

On the night of the speed dating session, Gisela arrives early to make sure everything is set up according to plan.

She is pleased to find the restaurant has cleared out a section of the building separated from the other half by a half-wall and some decorative archwork. The warm tones and bricks all around them give the modern diner a comfortable aura, and she's sure it will help to put her clients' minds at ease.

Auri shows up not long after her, and when she sees his tall frame walk toward her through the doorway, her heart leaps up to her throat.

His blue eyes find hers and she wonders briefly how awkward things will be between them. *Is he going to brush me off now that I've made everything weird? Do I give him the creeps all of a sudden?*

However, he flashes her one of those charming, wide smiles and pulls her into a warm hug as soon as he approaches.

"Gisela, Liebling," he murmurs, his mouth just behind her ear as he leans down to embrace her.

Shivers roll down her spine and she finds herself clinging helplessly to his chest. She can feel his firm muscles just underneath the navy blue dress shirt he is currently wearing, and a creeping warmth spreads across her body.

He pulls away all too soon and she blinks up at him. "Auri," she replies, her voice breathless. She clears her throat and looks away. "I'm glad you could make it tonight. I'm excited to see everybody's progress."

"Me too," he agrees. He presses a finger thoughtfully to his chin. "I just hope they don't act too… weird. Or out of place."

Gisela laughs as the tension melts from her chest. "I'm sure they'll be just fine. They've been showing a lot of promise recently." *How is it he can have me so on edge one second and so at ease the next?* She looks up at him and smiles; the nerves are evident in his expression as he chews at his bottom lip. She rests a hand gently against his arm and he glances down. His bright eyes glint with surprise before that familiar guardedness replaces it.

"I'm glad you think so," he breathes. They both evaluate their area of the restaurant.

There are ten small tables set with two chairs each and place settings for a couple. Everyone will sit where they like at the start of the night, long enough to order before beginning. Then, they will run through ten cycles of three-minute conversations, where the women will remain seated while the men switch between them. After they have finished, everyone will return to their original seating and enjoy their meals.

When the first few clients start shuffling in, Gisela and Auri exchange excited glances. All ten men were chosen from the foreigners, and all ten women were selected from the rest of her clientele base. Generally speaking, she chose a mixture of women who would be either gentle and understanding, critical and hesitant, or outspoken and self-assured. She wanted to gauge an overarching reaction to the men and their budding etiquette.

She observes with Auri from a table on the sidelines as servers take everyone's orders, and so far, things seem to be going smoothly.

That is until one of the servers approaches her with visible confusion written on his face.

"There are twenty guests here tonight, correct?" he asks immediately. He is holding a small notebook and tapping his foot nervously against the floor. "I noticed there are place settings for two at every table."

"Yes," Gisela says with a firm nod. She looks up at the clients. Each seat is filled. "Why do you ask?"

"Well, it's just…" He turns back to look at the crowd. "Some of the spots are empty. Maybe five or six?"

"What?"Gisela asks. She crosses her arms and blinks before looking again. Everyone is there. What is he on about?

"I'll handle it," Auri says abruptly. He strides out towards the tables.

"I'm sorry, ma'am," the server continues quickly. "I trust you are having a good night so far? Is this man your husband? Do you run Leben and Lieben together?"

She furrows her brow and stammers for a moment before answering. She tries to look around him, but now Auri is standing just in her line of vision enough to block most of the tables.

"Yes, I'm well," she answers. His last question suddenly registers, and it catches her off guard completely. She looks at him with wide eyes and blushed cheeks. "Oh! Uhm, no, I'm sorry. We aren't together." As she utters these words, she's slapped with a fresh wave of disappointment. *As much as I want to change that.*

"Oh, I'm sorry to assume, ma'am," he answers.

Just then, Auri walks back up and smiles at the server. "I just had to fetch some of them," he tells him. "They should all be there now."

"Thank you, sir," the server replies. He dips his head with a friendly smile before turning back and heading over to finish taking their orders.

Gisela eyes Auri with uncertainty as he slides into the booth across from her. "What was he talking about? They were all there," she says with bluntness.

He chuckles. "I know, I know. I think he's just... overwhelmed or something. Maybe tired. His mind is playing tricks on him."

"I guess so," Gisela replies. Still, she wonders if there is something there somehow beyond what she can see.

As the night proceeds and they finally start the speed dating session, Gisela forgets her worries and allows the giddiness to take over. Even more so than anything else she and Sophia have accomplished, this feels like the fruition of all her efforts. She's been working hard to integrate the foreign clients, and seeing them get along nicely with the others gives her a burst of renewed hope.

About halfway through the session, however, things start to turn south.

Lucien, the unusually vocal man she noticed when she first started teaching them, is present, and he has a few friends there as well. There are a few rounds where he talks over the woman he is matched with to joke and laugh obnoxiously across other tables with said friends.

The women exchange annoyed and distraught glances amongst each other, and Gisela can tell nobody is a fan of this behavior. It is completely souring the mood for everyone else.

She leaves the table to speak with Lucien at one point, but he brushes her off with a shrug and a laugh, then returns to his behavior.

Everything culminates when he actually stands up from one round and walks away. The woman at his table looks confused and actually starts to look frantically around the room as if she doesn't know where he went.

Strange, Gisela thinks. She watches Lucien walk towards another table. It's like she can't see him... like the server from earlier.

This happens a couple of other times with him and his friends, and Gisela finds her helpless frustration growing. She wants to get up and do something, but Auri encourages her to stay back and allow the event to run its course. He assures her that if she observes from a distance without being too active, she will be better able to tailor her feedback to everyone instead of focusing solely on the bad apples.

"He's being horrible and arrogant," Gisela huffs as once again Lucien stands up from his date. Thankfully, this is the last round and soon enough, everyone will return to their seats. "At least some of your friends are taking this seriously. I think a few of them even connected with a couple of the ladies."

"They aren't all my friends," Auri bites back.

She looks at him with alarm. There is something dark and stormy in his eyes as he glares, jaw clenched, out at the room. She can't tell where his gaze is directed, but it's obvious he doesn't feel too kindly about someone in that room.

Not soon enough, the speed dating is over and everyone can relieve the tension by enjoying their cuisine. Their meals were sponsored by the agency, and almost everyone has ordered steak or lobster. It feels good knowing they have room in the budget to spoil their clients now and again without worrying about losing funds.

The rest of the night passes without much incident, and by the time Gisela leaves, she feels exhausted but hopeful. Little does she know, there is more strife waiting for her before the week's end.

***

A few days later, Sophia is waiting in front of her office when she arrives in the morning. She is clutching a folded-up newspaper.

"What's going on?" Gisela asks slowly.

"Read over this," Sophia mutters. She presses the paper into Gisela's hands. "It sounds like your speed dating session had a few… kinks."

Gisela fumbles with the pages and takes a deep breath in as she skims over an article titled, "Leben and Lieben's first big move a flop?"

"A reporter was there," she breathes. "I knew I should have said or done something to Lucien. He was horrible to my women."

Sophia frowns and rubs a hand comfortingly on her shoulder.

The reporter writes about the servers bringing food to people who "weren't really there" and the puzzling experiences described by some of the women. It's noted they told the writer that some of the men would appear to vanish into thin air at times, conveniently only a minute or so into their conversation.

The article ends with:

> Not only did this so-called speed dating session come across as sketchy and confusing, with invisible diners and disappearing men, but the behavior of these foreigners was downright horrid. It seems Leben and Lieben has more to it than meets the eye. The question is this: Is it anything good?

Gisela feels her cheeks heat from anger and embarrassment. She crumples up the newspaper to Sophia's protest. *This is so weird,* she thinks. She can't pretend it wasn't strange when the server seemingly couldn't see some of her clients or when the women looked like their dates disappeared. She can't ignore these thoughts pressing into her mind, yet the indignation at this possible slight towards them simply for being foreigners screams loudly above them all.

"This is horrendous," she fumes, "she claims my clients 'weren't there.' Is it because they're foreigners? I didn't think Berlin was that prejudiced."

"I don't know," Sophia says slowly. She raises a brow. "To be honest, I've always gotten weird feelings about them. But it wasn't fair for her to publish this story without talking to you at all. Getting your thoughts or anything. She was obviously trying to stir things up."

Gisela nods. "Maybe we can get Monika to post something for us on social media to show our appreciation for our new clients. And to show them we aren't going to tolerate any slander."

Sophia smiles softly. "I'm sure she will," she replies. "For now, let's get some coffee in your system."

Chapter 15

Lessons and warnings

Monika does indeed create a post showing appreciation for Leben and Lieben's foreign clients, as well as a follow-up post explaining their process of instructing and guiding these foreigners through the local dating customs and social etiquette. Somehow, her skillful mind and clever wit manage to keep the posts sounding both humble and strong.

No less than a day after these posts are made, social media is abuzz with gossip and conversation about their agency. Much of it is still positive, with many influencers and Berlin locals praising them for their decisive action and explanation for the incident. For now, at least, it seems they have quelled the quickly growing flames that the infamous article sparked.

About a week later, though, all this falls to the back of Gisela's mind. She is meeting once again with her Oma, and it's the most nervous she recalls ever feeling before doing so.

She can't push back the memory of their last meeting, and she is certain her Oma will still act coldly toward her because of it. A part of her is surprised she even agreed to meet with her this month.

Still, she musters up her courage and keeps her appointment with Bast nonetheless.

She shows up at her door at the usual time, and Bast opens it up to let her in almost immediately. Just as Gisela suspected, the air around them is cordial but cool. Oma hardly says a word as she ushers her to the back room and hands her a cup of tea.

They sit together in silence for a few minutes, simply going through the motions of drinking their tea and beginning meditation. Once they have gone through the first cycle, however, Gisela cannot contain herself any longer.

"I need to talk to you," she blurts. Bast is just coming back to alertness after their twenty-minute meditation, and she blinks at Gisela rapidly with a creased brow. She doesn't say anything, though, opting instead to sip at her tea in silence, waiting.

In the span of about five minutes, Gisela word vomits everything to her. She spews out everything that has happened with the agency, the bizarre circumstances surrounding the foreign clients, and her budding feelings for Auri that have been rejected and encouraged in a never-ending cycle.

When she is finally done talking, she is nearly out of breath from spewing out her words. It feels as if she's just run a marathon or shifted out of her body like at their last meeting.

For a few minutes, Bast just sits in quiet contemplation. She takes her time absorbing this explosion of information before uttering a simple phrase: "Be careful."

"Careful?" Gisela asks. She places her hands on her knees and lets out a long sigh. "I'm sorry, what?" she tilts her head and grimaces. "That's all?"

Bast sighs and rests her forehead on her hand. "You're giving me a headache, girl," she complains. "Yes, that is mostly all. But about this Auri you mentioned." Her shoulders visibly tense and she sits up to fix Gisela with a frighteningly serious stare. "I will tell you one thing. Stay. Away."

Gisela's blood turns cold and she gulps the hard lump building in her throat. She opens her mouth to complain, but Bast fixes her with a glare so stern she shuts it immediately. She nods. "I can't promise that," she finally answers. Her stomach roils with shame and barely concealed anxiety, yet she feels proud of herself for standing up to her.

"Okay," Bast says with a wave of her hand. "That's all for today. You may go."

Gisela flinches, but she stands without protest and makes her way to the door. *Why did my mentioning Auri and the foreigners make her react that way? Is it just because she's still upset with me?* She leaves the houseboat without a word but for some reason, decides to linger outside the front door.

She doesn't know if it's intuition or coincidence, but something keeps her pressed against the door, listening and waiting with bated breath.

Within a minute, she hears Oma's faint voice. It sounds like she's on the phone with someone. "Yes," she says. "I'd like to have it delivered once a week, please…" She trails off and her voice grows softer as she moves through the house.

Suddenly, Gisela realizes what she is doing.

She's just ordered newspaper service. She frowns. *I just told her about that article, and now she's ordering the newspaper? What exactly is she planning? Is she going to just spy on me from afar? This is so weird, even for her.*

As she walks back home, she can't help the growing tightness in her chest. Something doesn't feel right, and until she understands the strange behavior of her Oma, she decides to keep her life much more private than she ever has.

***

Throughout that week, Gisela starts setting up the more promising clients from her foreigner group on matched dates. This is perhaps the most exciting part for her so far, as she can spend time analyzing their personalities and linking them to individuals she believes will fit well with them.

She logs data into the program, scans over the matches it suggests automatically, and inputs her own notes about observed personality traits and patterns in each client. She spends hours at a time sitting at her computer and adding new matches or removing some of the automated ones.

One of her favorite pairings is a couple of book lovers who, although they share a loved pastime, are so opposite in just about every single way. They weren't matched by the system initially, but from her personal observations of them, and her particular fondness for opposites attracting, she finds herself extremely intrigued by the possibility of them.

One is introverted; the other is extroverted. One is bubbly and friendly, the other more serious and demure. She hopes the outgoing man, one of the foreigners she approved to move forward in the program, will bring the shyer woman out of her shell and the woman will ground him and broaden his introspection.

She has also been setting aside time to stop in on some of her matches' first dates, just to see how things are doing. There have been a few flops, but most have been successful—especially her two book lovers.

She bumped into them at a cafe, where they were meeting up for a second date, and the chemistry between them could light up the whole building. They were beaming and glowing, and just as she imagined, the woman was growing more and more comfortable coming out of her shell.

This time-consuming yet satisfying process helps to take her mind off all the other worries crowding the back of her mind. The one at the forefront of those currently is the fact that Auri and Jurgen have been showing up at the office more than ever, and Auri has barely deflected his flirtation away from her the entire week.

If she hadn't felt confused and offended before, now she does.

Even more frustrating, he has asked her to set him up on an actual date. Begrudgingly, she obliges, hoping that seeing him whisk away some other woman will finally get her over him.

She is also feeling anxious about the men she chose to hold back in her program. Lucien is the main antagonizer of the three, and she's sure remediating his behavior will snap the others in line as well. He excels at instigating and leading the charge when it comes to rudeness and chauvinism, and she's not sure yet how to tackle those problems.

One day, she brings him and the others in for their first remedial lesson. She covers the topics of etiquette and social consideration once again, putting as much emphasis as she can on being considerate and respectful to someone even if you know you don't want to pursue them.

She makes sure to reprimand them for their behavior, too, explaining the negative effect it could have on L and L.

Near the end of their lesson, she sternly tells them, "If any of you continue with this behavior, I'll be forced to terminate your membership." She's addressing them all, but her stare lingers on Lucien. This comment alone seems to send him into a state of thoughtfulness, and he nods slowly at her with a serious expression.

Finally, she thinks, *something has gotten through his thick head.*

At the end of their lesson, he approaches her.

"So, Gisela," he begins. "I know we're technically in remediation, but I have a request."

She looks up at him with an arched eyebrow and crosses her arms. "Yes?" she asks.

"I want to be set up… with Monika."

"Monika?" She blinks. "Why?"

He shrugs, and his face breaks into a sly smirk. She's never thought about it before, but he has a sort of bad-boy attractiveness about him, with a chiseled jawline, dark hair, and dark blue eyes. His features are just as ethereal and perfect as Auri's but slightly less refined. "Do I need a reason?" He laughs. "I like her, okay?"

"You know, she isn't a client," Gisela huffs.

"Exactly," he confirms. "Which is why it doesn't matter that I'm in matchmaking limbo. Just talk to her for me, please? I know her, but not that well. I want you to put in a good word for me."

"I'm not sure there are—" She stops herself, and color floods into her cheeks. She was going to say, I'm not sure there are any good words for you, but this would have been exceptionally harsh, so she's glad she caught herself. She takes a breath. "I'm not sure she'll agree to it." Her guilt gets the better of her when she remembers what she almost said. "But okay… I'll talk to her."

"Yes! Thank you, Gisela!" He grins and pulls her in to press a hasty kiss on her cheek. "Bye-bye now!"

She watches, mystified, as he practically bounds out the door.

Hopefully, Monika and Hans really do have something going on, she muses, *and she'll turn him down immediately. I do not have a good feeling about this one.*

Chapter 16

Vexing or vixen

One Friday evening, Gisela is looking over her plans to see which couple she can check up on this time. It's become a habit of hers to go every Friday night for a couple of weeks now, and when she reads the names listed for this particular night, her heart drops.

This first date is Auri's.

She paired him off with a woman named Louisa, who seems fairly friendly and outgoing, with a great sense of humor. Truthfully, she had a difficult time putting much thought into this match. She mostly found herself relying on the system.

She sighs as she looks over the matchmaking program. She scrolls up and down the list of matches several times before resigning to the fact that there are simply no other dates tonight. She groans and drops her head against the desk.

I don't have to go, she tells herself. *It's not like this is some commitment I made. And I don't think Auri would care if I dropped by.* Still, some part of herself she assumes must be masochistic is yelling at her to suck it up and drop by anyway. *It is on my way home. I suppose I'd have to go out of my way to avoid it.* She sighs and slowly sits up.

She then pulls out a compact from her tote bag and sets to touching up her makeup. *If I'm going to intrude on my crush's first date, I better at least look nice,* she rationalizes. The thought is mildly amusing, yet she tries to ignore the truthfulness behind it.

Sophia opens up her door to poke her head in and say goodnight. "You look nice," she comments. "Going somewhere?"

"Oh, just checking on Auri and his date," she replies nonchalantly.

Sophia chortles. "Okay, babe, have fun with that." She shakes her head and ducks back out.

Even Sophia is over this mess, she ponders. *Maybe that should be a sign.* Still, she finds herself drawn to the roll-around clothing rack she keeps in her office. The clothes displayed there are mostly decorative; she's been filling it with beautiful, fancy dresses she's purchased since they opened L and L. So far, she only has three. But she doesn't wear clothes like this often, so she chooses to admire them from a distance.

Until tonight.

This is silly, she thinks. Still, she pulls a velvet midi dress off a hanger and gazes at its lovely, structured mermaid hem and corset-style bodice. The straps are thin and delicate, and they tie into bows at the tops of her shoulders. Before she can even register what she is doing, the dress is on her body.

And when she looks at herself in the mirror, she watches her own smile grow. *Perfect,* she thinks. *Tonight I will know one thing for sure. Is Auri really attracted to me?*

***

When Gisela arrives at the up-and-coming, modern restaurant she had arranged for Auri and his date to dine at, she is dismayed and confused to find him sitting outside on a bench.

He is at the front of the restaurant, and she almost doesn't notice him as she approaches the door. When a group of people walks inside, clearing the space around her, the first things she notices are his long legs stretched out in front of him.

She would recognize his tall build anywhere; it catches her eye, even when he is hunched over on a bench with his head in his hands. Every time she looks at him, it's easy to see why so many other women walking by make a double-take in his direction.

His long, silvery hair is striking; it connotes prominence and elegance. He is tall and slender but obviously strong by the way his suits are always perfectly tailored to fit snugly against his toned arms and chest.

Aside from his appearance, Gisela can't explain the pull she feels to him, as if the one man meant perfectly for her has finally walked into her life and there's no way she can ever let him go.

Her eyes go wide and she stares, open-mouthed for a moment before slowly backing away from the entrance.

Her heart pounds in her ears, and when her mouth finally closes, it twists into a frown. She can't tell if she is excited to see him here alone or worried because of his despondence. *As guilty as it makes me feel, I think it's a bit of both,* she realizes.

She sucks in a deep breath and takes a few steps toward him. He doesn't even look up until she is sitting on the bench beside him.

His long hair cascades around his head, shielding his expression, and she has to fight herself to keep from running her hands across it. It is pulled half-back with some kind of ornate clip that fascinates her, and its sleek texture gleams in the glow of the streetlight.

After a minute, though, he turns to peer up at her. His normally bright, lively eyes are dull and unfocused. As soon as he registers who she is, they blink a few times and the guardedness returns.

He sits up straight, back practically snapping with the speed of his movement. "Gisela," he greets, "how nice it is to see you here… what *are* you doing here?"

She smiles softly. "I was just… on my way home. And I decided to drop by to see how your date was going. How is it going? Or, should I ask, is it going?"

He lets out a short chuckle before looking away.

"Well, she showed up here, took about one look at me, and walked away."

"What?" Gisela stammers.

"Maybe she thought I was too… unusual looking? I'm sure you've noticed me and my friends don't exactly look quite the same as your people." He leans back and crosses his arms behind his shoulders, linking his hands together to rest his head against. His pale blue eyes, darker now in the dim light, stare up toward the sky with a sense of wistfulness.

"You may be a little unusual," Gisea admits, "but I would say you are unusually attractive. Much more so than any other man I've seen here in Berlin."

He smirks and looks over at her with a raised eyebrow.

"I've had to deal with that sort of thing and weird looks my whole life," she continues. "People were always put off by me for some reason. I think it also has to do with my disposition. I've heard I can be rather blunt."

He laughs louder this time, and as he shakes his head with a grin, she finds her cheeks lighting up with one of her own. Just seeing his mood lift and those dark clouds start to drift away fills her with elation.

"I appreciate that about you," he says earnestly. He sets his arms down on either side of him and looks at her. "Maybe this night shouldn't be wasted. Would you like to go on a walk?"

"Yes," she replies immediately.

He smiles at her, stands, and offers his hand for her to take. She presses her hand gently in his and he pulls her to her feet with ease. When she is finally upright, his eyes rake appreciatively over her body. They grow wider with each passing second, and she could swear she can see the breath leave his lungs.

"Wow…" he mutters. He looks back into her eyes, his expression as unreadable as ever. "You look absolutely stunning, Gisela, my Liebling."

Her heartbeat speeds up at the sound of her tender pet name. She can't explain it, but hearing her name alone spill from his lips, let alone attached to such a sweet title, sets butterflies loose in her stomach.

"This old thing?" she says with a laugh, looking down to try and disguise the blush rising to her cheeks. She looks back up and brushes a lock of hair behind her ear. "Do you want to walk to my house? You can come in for a drink if you'd like."

Something in his gaze darkens, and her stomach does a backflip.

"I'd love that," he purrs. He crowds her space and presses a hand to the small of her back. "Let's go, Liebling."

***

As they walk together in the moonlight, Gisela finds herself feeling lighter and lighter. They chat easily and laugh, and the entire time his touch never strays from her. At times he keeps his hand steady against her back and at certain points, their arms loop together.

They stop now and then to look at the sky and admire the stars. Auri speaks with wistfulness and something that almost sounds like nostalgic musing as he talks about planets far, far, away and their names.

Although Gisela appreciated seeing a more vulnerable side of him, even if it was short-lived, she is glad to see his mood so quickly uplifted.

When they finally reach her front step, the quiet buzz of nervousness that's been building slowly the entire time has reached an all-time high. Her face feels flushed and even though she hasn't exerted herself at all, she is almost out of breath.

She tries not to let herself expect too much from this visit, but she can't help the hope that is burrowing itself deeper and deeper in her heart.

Surely men and women mostly go to each other's houses for a drink late at night for one reason. And with the way he looked at me before… Is Auri finally going to make a move on me?

She lets them inside and leads him to the kitchen, where she pours them both a healthy glass of merlot. Her cat, Oliver, follows them happily and winds himself around their legs as they chat.

Auri seems particularly amused by him as he crouches down to pet him a few times and speaks to him in soft, gentle tones.

They continue their conversation, but as they sip at their wine and stand side by side at the island, something tense and unspoken hangs in the air between them.

"I'm sorry your date was a miss," she mumbles. "If you want, I can look for somebody else for you tomorrow." She turns to face him. "You are… incredible, Auri. Any woman would be fortunate to have you."

He draws closer until he is standing mere inches away and she feels as if each breath she takes in is one he's exhaled.

His eyes stare into hers, searching. He smiles, but not the same lighthearted grin he shows to everyone and anyone. It is a closed-mouth smile, slow, genuine, and distracted.

"Thank you, Liebling," he whispers back. "I don't think I'm looking to date anyone now, though. I've realized something tonight."

"You have?" she asks. Her breath hitches and she eases closer until their chests almost touch. Warmth emanates off of him, and the tug she feels is almost irresistible, like gravity forcing her nearer.

He nods, and his eyes glance briefly to her lips.

"Auri, I have to ask you something," she murmurs. Her cheeks are burning now, and she's struggling to get out her words. She's never felt intensity or heat like this, heat that spreads like wildfire through her whole body. "Why have you been treating me like you do? Flirting and messing with me only to turn me away?"

"Gisela…" He trails off and gulps. "I don't… I don't want anything serious right now."

"I'm okay with casual," she lies quickly, hoping he won't see through it. Truthfully, she doesn't want to be casual. Not with him. She doesn't think she could be casual with him. But she'll say anything right now to get his lips on hers.

"You deserve more," he whispers. But he leans down. His mouth is only centimeters away, and he is setting his wine glass on the counter. Her blood is roaring in her ears now and everything within her is consumed by this moment.

"I want you," she answers.

A low growl resounds in his throat, and suddenly his mouth crashes into hers.

Their lips move together as naturally as lava and smoke, and she practically slams her own glass down to thread her fingers into those enticing blonde locks. His hair is just as soft as it looks, and as his hands grip her waist, she lets out a gasp into his mouth.

His lips are soft and insistent all at once, both firm and yielding against her own. The kiss deepens as seconds pass, each one feeling like an eternity and yet not long enough.

As suddenly as it started, though, it ends, and he pulls away with a gasp. She presses a finger to her swollen lips, and her eyes grow wide. She can still taste him, sweet like cherries, with the smokiness of the wine still lingering there.

"Gisela, Liebling," he says, this time with a firmness. He squeezes her waist, and the sensation sends a jolt all the way through her. "I'm sorry, but I really can't. I care about you. As a friend. I don't want to hurt you."

"Auri," she starts, a protest already on her lips.

"No, I'm sorry," he interrupts. He slowly pulls away and creates more distance between them.

"Why are you doing this?" she asks, voice strained. She can feel moisture pressing in the corners of her eyes. Her feelings are warring within her, each one struggling for dominance, and she feels overwhelmed completely.

She backs out of the kitchen and grasps at her scalp. She turns around and walks out of the room, fighting back her tears as they threaten to spill out. "Why do you lead me on?" she shouts. "Auri, this thing is tormenting me."

He follows her, catching up quickly and spinning her around to press her into his chest.

"Gisela, Liebling, I'm sorry," he replies. "I'm so sorry. I was carried away. We both were. I'm just not ready for this. I didn't mean to lead you on."

"Why did you say that earlier?"

"Say what?" he asks.

"The thing you said about realizing why you don't want to date anybody."

He curses under his breath, but the word doesn't sound like any language she's ever heard. "I shouldn't have said it like that," he admits. "I'm sorry. I just meant that I want to focus on helping my friends before working on myself. I mean, I'm not even thirty yet."

Gisela lets out a short laugh, thinking he's joking, but quickly stops when she realizes he isn't. *That sounds backward,* she muses.

"I'm just not in a place in my life, in my journey, to have a relationship yet. And I can already tell there would be no casual between us," he explains. "I'm sorry, Gisela. I can leave now if you want."

She sighs and pulls begrudgingly from his grip. "I've never felt a connection so strong and so fast as I do with you," she admits.

He meets her gaze and lets out a long breath.

"But I understand. Well, I don't," she continues. This time he does laugh, and she feels slightly reassured to see his smile return. "But I'll respect what you want. And you don't have to go. Stay in the guest room. It's late, and you just drank that giant glass of wine. I think we could both use some sleep."

He smiles with a nod. "Thank you, Gisela, my Liebling."

The sound of this nickname still causes her heart to leap to her throat, and she smiles.

It feels ridiculous to hold out hope, she thinks. But when he calls me that, I can't help it. Maybe one of these days, he'll finally give in to us.

Chapter 17

Interest from an unexpected source

Gisela tosses and turns all night, her dreams plagued by strange sensations and voices that seem to beckon her toward them insistently. Each time she wakes up, she can't remember whose voice called to her, but she knows it was someone familiar. It feels as if somebody is reaching out to touch her, but she's not quite within their grasp. She wonders if this is how her Oma felt when she was reaching out to her from outside her body.

The next morning when Gisela awakens with the sunrise, Oliver is curled up beside her. She smiles and rubs her hand fondly over his striped flank. He lifts his head to look at her with half-lidded eyes and sleepily begins grooming his paw.

Gisela ventures out of her room with one thought on her mind. When she checks the guest room, she finds Auri has already left.

Her stomach swells with disappointment, yet she is not surprised. He has made the bed and left the room possibly even tidier than it was before, and she doesn't know whether to feel charmed or amused.

She touches her mouth as she stares into the room, and the thought of their kiss the night before sends a thousand butterflies ricocheting within her. She's had her decent share of kisses, but none quite as resounding as that one.

She takes in a deep breath, still lingering on the feeling of his warm lips and his hands on her waist. *How am I going to get anything done today?* she wonders. Still, she starts her morning routine nonetheless and gets ready to meet up with Mia for a light jog.

They spend most of the run in companionable silence, like usual, but towards the end, Mia confides in her about her recent time spent with

Jurgen. She doesn't mention their escapade the night of the house party, but Gisela ponders on it with amusement. Apparently, they've gone on a couple of dates now and he has been the perfect gentleman.

Gentleman isn't normally a word I'd assign to him, she muses. Still, she is glad her friend is happy, even if she feels a slight tug of jealousy in her stomach. She decides not to share about her encounter with Auri, as she doesn't want to sour the mood or focus the attention back on herself.

Still, she carries her feelings with her in private even after they part ways, and even as she lays in bed that night, she can't tear her mind away from that cursed kiss.

***

When the new work week begins, Gisela is dismayed and a bit annoyed to find they have a new regular visitor. Even with her conflicting feelings and sore pride, she finds herself wishing Auri was still hanging out because, this time, it's Lucien.

She tells him every day he doesn't need to be there all the time, considering she only hosts remedial lessons for him and the others once a week. Still, he chooses to loiter. Occasionally he makes himself helpful, bringing her coffee and tidying up the space.

The weirdest part of all, though, is she's pretty sure he's been flirting with her.

Every time they interact, he's either showering her with over-the-top compliments, trying to make her laugh with crude jokes, or teasing her incessantly. Considering she isn't interested in him in the slightest, it makes him all the more aggravating.

She tries to ignore the fact that deep down, the attention is somewhat flattering.

On Thursday afternoon, she is taking a short break with a hot cup of coffee in the break room. She is reading a new book, enjoying her few minutes of silence, and hoping with all her might that he won't walk through that door.

Naturally, he appears in the doorway after only five minutes.

She has to suppress the groan that rises up her throat when she looks up at him. *Maybe he'll go away if I ignore him,* she muses. She gives him a polite smile and returns to her reading.

He doesn't get the hint. Instead, he pulls out the chair beside her with a loud scraping noise, turns it around backward, and sits with his legs on either side of it and his arms across the back.

His stare bores into her for a few seconds before he says, "I've been hoping to get you alone all day, Gisela. If I didn't know any better, I'd say you've been avoiding me."

"Why bother?" she retorts. "I know you'd hunt me down, so why even try?"

"Ouch," he says with a low whistle, playfully smacking his chest and leaning back with a dramatic sigh. "That hurts."

"You should probably see a doctor then," she snaps.

"I'll consider it. But I think he might tell me I'm suffering from a case of lovesickness."

"Oh please," she sighs. "What?"

He laughs and brushes his hand against her arm. "Lighten up; I'm just messing with you. What are you reading?"

"Nothing currently," she says, fixing him with a pointed look. "I was reading this autobiography, though. Maybe you should try your hand at reading sometime. Have you ever tried it?"

He laughs again, so loud it fills the room. "Someone is feeling witty today. How can you be so grouchy with coffee in your hands?"

She raises an eyebrow at him and he laughs again before shrugging. "Point taken. Anyway, I just have a question for you. Then I promise I'll leave you alone."

She slides her bookmark into the book and shuts it before directing her attention to Lucien. "Yes?" she asks.

"Will you go out with me?" he asks. He brushes a hand nervously through his dark hair, and those stormy blue eyes seem surprisingly earnest.

"What?" she exclaims. She blinks at him rapidly and crinkles her forehead. "Are you messing with me? I thought you wanted to go out with Monika."

He shrugs. "Well, I guess the past few weeks, you've just caught my eye even more."

She groans and presses her head into her palm.

"I'm sorry, Lucien, but I'm sort of…" She searches for the right words, doubt creeping up as the image of Auri comes to the forefront of her mind. She wants to say she's figuring things out with someone else, but truthfully she doesn't know where things are heading with him.

"Sort of…?" Lucien pushes. "Sort of anything doesn't sound strong enough to say no, in my opinion," he adds with a laugh.

She raises an eyebrow and gives him an arch look. "I'm interested in someone else," she says bluntly. *God, I hope he'll leave me alone.*

"Who?" he demands, slapping his hand on the table. "I'll challenge him. I'll knock him out. Just say his name and we'll get it squared away."

What is he talking about? Challenge? Knock him out?

"Are you listening?" she snaps. "I don't want to date you, Lucien. I'll get you a date with Monika if you really want, but this," she gestures between them, "is *never* gonna happen."

His smile immediately twists into a scowl, and he jolts from his seat, loudly scraping his chair on the floor in the process. "Fine," he bites out, "please, get me a date with Monika. It's probably her anyway." With that, he storms from the room.

"Probably her?" she mutters to herself, shaking her head. "What does that even mean? Why are these people so weird?"

After a long moment of confused contemplation, she sighs and opens up her book. "Maybe I can just pretend it never happened and forget about it all," she mumbles. She happily returns to her reading, choosing to push all her complicated questions to the back of her mind.

***

Later that evening, she shoots Monika a text asking if she can meet with her at the agency. Thankfully, she agrees. Gisela feels as if she can't put off telling her about Lucien's interest any longer. She has to get it off her chest to someone and doesn't want to burden Sophia with it when she's already weirded out by the foreigners enough.

Her motives aren't entirely unselfish, either; she feels that the sooner she's able to get Lucien off of her tail, the better.

So when Monika strolls into her office just a few minutes after closing time, a look of open curiosity on her face, Gisela launches into the news almost instantly.

"Lucien wants me to set you two up on a date."

Monika freezes in her steps, and her face blanches for just a moment. "W-what?" she stammers.

She is normally so confident and collected, Gisela can only wonder if this response is in part due to whatever is brewing between her and Hans.

"He's been pestering me for almost two weeks," Gisela groans. Monika slowly slides into the seat across from her desk. "He really wants me to talk to you and ask if you'll go out with him."

Monka's face breaks into a grin and she laughs loudly. "That's hilarious!" she wheezes out between her cackles.

Gisela smirks. She isn't surprised by this rejection; Monika would never put up with Lucien's cocky attitude and flaming ego. "So I take it that's a no?" she inquires, holding in laughter of her own.

"Did you ever think it would be otherwise?" Monika questions, bemused.

"Nope," Gisela responds, shaking her head in wide swings. "I know you too well."

"I knew Lucien…" Monika pauses mid-sentence and something uncertain flashes in her eyes before she continues. "A while. I guess you could say he was a family friend. You remember when my family would make those trips a few times a year, right? When we were growing up?"

Gisela nods. "You were going back to your parents' homeland, right?"

Monika smiles softly. "Yes," she replies. Her gaze becomes distant, as if she is reminiscing on a place she holds dearly. The moment is short, though, and she clears her throat before continuing. "Anyway, Lucien and some of the others you met would hang out with Jurgen and me a lot of the time. And he's always been the way he is."

"A bit of an ass?" Gisela interrupts, laughter in her voice.

"Yes," Monika says, biting back her own laugh. "A bit of an ass." Her smile then turns into a frown. "He sort of turned down… a different path than the rest of us."

"What do you mean?"

Monika shuffles in her seat, appearing as if she isn't sure how to say what she truly wants to. For a second, her expression softens, and Gisela thinks she is about to reveal some well-kept secret. But at the last second, her walls return, and she replies, "He just moved away from everyone and got mixed up with the wrong men for a while. But I hope he's back on the right path now."

Gisela nods, and although she's glad Monika is finally telling her a bit more about that mysterious homeland she used to travel to, she feels as if her guardedness is not unlike Auri or Bast's. She can't help feeling crestfallen. *Must all the people I care about keep secrets from me? At least Sophia is always honest.*

She decides to change the subject to get her mind off these maddening topics. "So you *really* won't go on *one* date with him?" Gisela presses. She pushes her face into her desk. "He's been driving me crazy. He even asked *me* out today. Can you believe it?"

Monika laughs. "Yes, actually. He probably views you as a challenge of some sort. You can be a bit of a tough one to crack, Gisela."

"I don't buy it," she quips. She begins chewing on her lip, though. *Am I really? Is that why hardly any man has ever expressed interest in me? And why Auri can't seem to give in to whatever is happening between us?*

Monika pauses for a moment before going on. "You and I are both intimidating," she adds. "Just in different ways. You speak your mind, mostly unashamedly. And I think that can intimidate the insecure people around you."

Gisela blinks before sitting up and eyeing Monika with curiosity. "Thank you," she murmurs, "for your honesty. I appreciate it."

"As I appreciate yours," Monika replies quickly. But that same uncertain look flashes in her eyes again, and Gisela wonders if she isn't being as honest as she wants to be.

What could be holding her back? she wonders.

"And fine," Monika says with a sigh. "I will… go out with him. Give me his number, and I'll text him later."

Gisela grins and quickly pulls up her client database before sending his contact info to Monika.

I couldn't be more intrigued to see how this plays out.

Chapter 18

Nothing but smoke here

At the start of the next week, Gisela walks to work on Monday morning with a strange sense of unease settled over her.

She doesn't know why, but the entire time she's walking there, it feels as if something bad is going to happen. When she reaches Leben and Lieben, she begins to unlock the front door when she feels the hairs on the back of her neck stand on edge.

When she whips around, she notices a slightly familiar-looking woman lingering in the doorway of a shop across the street. She has long blonde hair swept up in a claw clip against the back of her head, and there is a camera slung around her neck. She is eyeing Gisela suspiciously, but when their eyes meet, she looks away.

It's a bit strange, considering the boutique she's loitering near doesn't open for another half hour. *I suppose she could be waiting there. But why the camera? Am I just losing it? She could be a photographer or something, waiting to meet with some clients. Who knows?*

The woman is dressed in black from head to toe, so Gisela resigns to the thought that she's probably a photographer after all and heads inside.

Sophia arrives not long after her, and they proceed with their workdays like usual. There is an upbeat aura radiating through the whole building, as numbers have been steadily rising, even after the speed dating incident, and profits are already booming.

The money doesn't matter much to Gisela, though; what matters is she feels more fulfilled with her life than she ever has before. And she's happy to see her best friend feeling the same way.

However, the next time Gisela looks out the front windows when she is fixing some floral arrangements displayed on a table in the front, she notices that same blonde woman from the morning.

Her blood chills. *She's still there?* Obviously, this woman wasn't a normal photographer or somebody waiting outside for a shop to open. No, this person has a goal. She is across the street, scribbling something in a notebook.

After a moment, she lifts up her camera and turns it around, seemingly looking through its pictures.

Gisela stares as she mindlessly arranges the flowers in their pot. *This is getting kind of… creepy.*

Suddenly, the strange woman looks towards the window, and for the second time that day, their eyes meet. She gives Gisela a tight-lipped smile and a nod before walking away.

She's glad the mystery woman is gone, but Gisela can't shake the feeling deep down she hasn't seen the last of her yet.

***

Throughout the week, Gisela keeps seeing the same woman with the camera outside their building, taking pictures and writing down notes. However, she doesn't approach. Sophia is itching to confront her, but they're both too weirded out by her behavior to do so.

However, on Friday morning Sophia practically runs into Gisela's office; she slams open the door and bolts towards her desk, holding out her cell phone.

"*Look,*" she says, teeth clenched. "It's her. The woman outside."

Gisela looks at her phone and notices the browser is open to the local newspaper's website. "Oh my gosh," she mutters. The woman's picture is attached to a name.

Roxanne Philpot. The writer of that seething article directed at Leben and Lieben.

"She's a reporter," Gisela breathes. "I can't believe I didn't think of that sooner." She stands up, nearly knocking over her chair in the process. "Let's go talk to her."

Conveniently, Roxanne is opening their door just as they walk through the front lobby. The tiny bell above it rings, a little too late to warn them of her presence.

"Roxanne," Gisela says, trying to keep any kind of social advantage she can. So far, this lady hasn't posed a direct threat, but she certainly doesn't bode good tidings for their agency. "How are you today? I've noticed you watching our establishment a lot this past week. Get any good pictures? We'd love to post some on our website." Her words fly out faster than she can think, and she hardly recognizes her own assertiveness.

Sophia looks impressed, though, with a pleased smile on her lips and arms folded across her chest.

Roxanne's eyes go wide for a second before she plasters on a smile that doesn't quite reach her eyes. "Ladies, good morning." She holds her arms out as she speaks. "Well, now that you probably know why I'm here, we can skip all the pleasantries. I was hoping to get a few minutes of your time to conduct an interview with one of you. Would that be possible today?"

Gisela turns to Sophia, who is visually bristling. Her jaw is clenched and her throat is strained, judging by the vein popping out of it. *There's no way I could throw Sophia into a room with this lady. I'll have to do it.*

"Okay," she says, "I will let you interview me. I will give you about fifteen minutes to prepare yourself and then you may meet me in my office."

"Oh, I'm prepared," Roxanne answers quickly.

"I'm sure you'll find something to do, then," Gisela replies, voice cold as steel. "See you in fifteen. You can stay inside if you'd like."

Roxanne gives her that same tight smile from the other day and Gisela returns with Sophia back to her office.

"That was bad*ass*," Sophia hisses with a grin as soon as they slip inside. "You kept control of the situation. Nice thinking."

"Honestly, I wasn't really thinking," Gisela admits. She takes a deep breath. "But thank you. We should probably figure out what we're going to do now."

"Don't freak out," Sophia says. "That's easy for me to say since you're the one who's conducting the interview. But just answer her questions without giving away information about our clients. Tell her they have a right to privacy. Say something generic like… you appreciate all of your clients and you are giving them room to grow in the social realm."

"Wow, Soph," Gisela teases, "that was good. Maybe you should be in the interview."

Sophia laughs but Gisela quirks an eyebrow at her. "Are you serious?" She practically squeaks. "That lady is intimidating."

"So am I," Gisela says, straightening her back as she looks back on the words Monika spoke to her the other day. *"You speak your mind, mostly unashamedly. And I think that can intimidate the insecure people around you."*

"Sit in on the interview with me," Gisela adds. "She can't come waltzing in here making demands. A team of two is stronger than one. And if she has a problem with that… she can always leave."

Sophia's lips turn up into a smile, and she crinkles her nose affectionately at Gisela. "This is why I love you," she jokes, smacking her hand playfully against her back. "She won't know what hit her."

When they leave her office to pull Roxanne in, Gisela is surprised to hear her exchanging words with someone, and she would recognize the deep voice anywhere.

"Why is Auri here?" she mumbles. She doesn't know if she should be thrown off or comforted, but having his presence there is oddly reassuring. They walk into the lobby to see Auri has just walked in and is simply being polite with Roxanne.

"You are the connection between Leben and Lieben and the group of foreigners, then?" Roxanne asks him, eyes glinting. "Would you like to tell me more about that?" She is sitting comfortably in an armchair with her legs crossed and pen at the ready.

"I see you've met Auri," Gisela interrupts. She greets them both with a smile. "He has been incredibly helpful in teaching and coordinating all of my lessons with our foreign clients. If you're as ready as you said, we can take you in for that interview now."

Auri looks over at her, eyebrows creased with worry. "Should I sit in?" he asks.

Gisela shakes her head. "That's okay. We can handle this."

Roxanne gives her a stiff nod and follows her and Sophia into the office.

When she realizes neither of them is leaving, she frowns slightly before sitting down in the chair across from Gisela's desk. Sophia sits in a chair beside Gisela.

They start the interview with a few casual, fairly lighthearted questions about the two of them and why they started Leben and Lieben. They explain their backstory of working in marketing together, their friendship since college, their dreams of doing something bigger, and the main events that culminated in them starting this business.

"I love people," Gisela adds. "I especially love figuring them out and what makes them tick. I studied sociology in school and doing this work really gives me a sense of fulfillment nothing else has."

"Lovely," Roxanne says with a smile. It doesn't quite reach her eyes, though, and she clears her throat before moving on. "Would you be able to tell me why you started working with the group of foreigners your friend Auri has brought over?"

"Oh, well…" Gisela pauses.

"Partially because it was simply a good business deal," Sophia jumps in. She holds out her hands. "I'm the numbers gal around here. We saw an opportunity to expand not only our client base almost right away after opening but expand our company's offerings. Perhaps in the future, once we've worked out some of the kinks in this program, we can offer other classes to help clients out with social etiquette and navigating the dating world. It can be a scary place for many, not just foreigners."

Roxanne opens her mouth for a moment before shutting it and scribbling something down. She has a tense smile on, but it seems she hasn't gotten exactly what she's looking for yet.

"You said you're still… working out kinks in the program? Could that have to do with your foreign clients' unruly behavior at your speed dating event the other night?" she asks. She looks at both of them with scrutinizing brown eyes.

"Well, you should have seen them when they first started their lessons," Gisela replies. "They've come a long way. Most of them were perfectly well-behaved, and the outbursts from the others were entirely unexpected. As our first event mixing them with other clients, it was the first time we've seen them interact in a setting like that. However, we do have the clients who acted out participating in mandatory remedial lessons, while the others have moved on."

"Exactly," Sophia cuts in, "we are taking every step to make sure everybody is treated with respect and making this an opportunity for growth and learning. Isn't it good we decided to make their first dates public in an event like this rather than send them out with individual matches?"

Roxanne takes in a deep breath, seeming to gather whatever pressing question she can wring out. She hesitantly writes a few more notes on her notepad.

"Would you be willing to share the names of those clients you've put in remedial lessons?" she asks. "I'm sure the public, and any potential matches you may assign them to, would like to know these things in the future."

Gisela furrows her brow. "No," she says firmly. "Our client's information is confidential."

"These aren't dangerous people," Sophia urges. "At worst, just a bit rude. Like we said, we are working to remediate that."

"So you don't care about the public, then? Or other clients? Why do you place so much favor on these… foreigners, who contribute nothing to our town or to Berlin?"

Gisela's face flushes in anger. "Of course, we care about our clients," she snaps. "And the fact that these ones happen to be foreign doesn't change anything. We are thankful for them. We're thankful for all our clients. And we're pleased to have them with us."

"Are you sure there aren't any… personal matters influencing the way you run your business?" Roxanne leans forward with a small smirk on her face. "This gentleman Auri… he's more than just a business partner to you, isn't he, Ms. Gisela?"

Gisela gapes. She fidgets in her seat and stammers before looking at Sophia. But her friend is just as much at a loss as she is. She clenches her fists. "Let's keep this on topic," she finally seethes.

"Oh, but we are on topic," Roxanne insists. She sits back and starts scribbling furiously. "You seem rather defensive about this. Perhaps you've come upon some large sum of money from working with these clients, enough to look past their potential dangers? Or maybe you are favoring them more because Mr. Auri has found his way into your—"

"Enough." A deep, resounding voice comes from the open office door. He is soft-spoken, but the firm timbre in his words commands every single drop of their attention.

His arms are crossed at his chest, and a flickering fire is in his normally bright eyes. "I think you should leave, Ms. Roxanne," he practically growls. "You have no business here."

She starts to protest, but Auri fixes her with a pointed look that seems to change the entire essence of her demeanor. Instantly, her shoulders slack and her face becomes impassive. She nods, picks up her things, and walks out without a word.

"Wait," Auri calls as she approaches the lobby. She stills. "Throw out your notepad," he adds. She nods again and tosses the book into the nearest trash can.

Sophia gasps. Gisela clenches the arms of her chair. *What the hell? How is he doing that?*

Roxanne leaves with a gentle slam of the front door, and the building is enclosed in silence. Gisela stares up at Auri, unable to form any words. A feeling of warmth seeps through her body, regardless of the bizarre circumstances. *He stood up for me. For us.* She breathes a deep sigh of relief. No matter how strange his behavior is, it feels nice to be protected by him.

"What was that?" Sophia shrieks. "How'd you just—she just," she stops and breathes in and out. "How did you get her to just leave, let alone toss out her notes?"

Auri looks back at them and shrugs, but it's obvious he's hiding something. "Dumb luck, I guess," he kids. "I knew I came here for a reason today. I just didn't know why…" He trails off and looks back towards the lobby, thoughtfulness glazing over his expression. "Have a good day, ladies."

And just like that, he leaves.

Gisela doesn't realize until now how her heart is hammering in her chest, and her mouth is dry. She isn't sure if it's because of that stressful interview or Auri's rescue. Either way, she is entirely unsettled. *Who really is Auri, anyway? What is he hiding?*

Chapter 19

Gisella does a word vomit

The weeks that pass after the incident with Roxanne only get weirder and weirder. Gisela has officially passed Lucien's friends to the next phase of their journey since they've displayed immense growth during their remedial lessons. Therefore, she's matched all of them at least once or twice already, and the rest of the foreigners have gotten even more dates already.

Some of them seem to be doing really well, with a few even finding matches that suit them incredibly and going on more than one date.

Others, however, are not quite there yet.

Their program has a feature where clients can actually review their dates—confidentially, of course. Slowly, reviews start coming in from their other clients, complaining about being matched with "weirdos" and "creeps." Gisela isn't sure what to do about it, so she decides to send an email about all of it to Monika and Mia, asking for advice on what to do.

Now that Gisela doesn't have to plan and teach any lessons, she has a lot more free time on her hands.

One afternoon, she finds herself musing on Sophia's words from their interview. *Maybe it would be a good idea to start hosting lessons for other potential clients. We could do month-long courses, where we allow people to sign up and attend a lesson once or twice a week. We can do fun activities, too, like I did with the foreigners, but I'll tailor them a bit differently for the locals. And then we could even explore having another speed dating session.*

She continues pondering on these ideas for a few minutes until she decides to open a few documents and start typing out ideas, notes, and ways to implement them.

A few hours later, she has pages upon pages detailing all of her current ideas for Leben and Lieben, complete with her plans for more lessons as well as things like monthly speed dating nights hosted at the agency, trivia nights, drinks, and dancing with live bands, and a few other fun events to spoil their clients with.

These will really make us stand out from any other agency, she thinks to herself. *I can only see L and L getting bigger as time goes on. Maybe one day we could even franchise…* She pauses for a moment, then frowns and shakes her head. "Nah," she says out loud, "I don't think I want that." She then smiles to herself and starts humming as she gets back to work.

Suddenly, in the middle of typing, a small notification pops up in the corner of her computer screen. She halts her movements and glances up at it. When she reads the preview, her heart drops.

Client dropping out of system…

She hurriedly clicks on the notification box, pulling up the L and L system to read a short and polite message written to her by one of their clients.

For a second, she hopes this person is only leaving because she's found success, but that is not the case. She is leaving because of her matches.

Apparently, she's only ever been matched with foreigners, and every single one of them has been rude and disrespectful. After skimming the rest of the message, Gisela finds out she has become increasingly disappointed and no longer feels safe giving Leben and Lieben her business.

She frowns at the monitor. "How can this happen?" she breathes. Just as she's clicking away from the message, another notification pops up with the same exact preview text. "No, no, no." she gasps as she clicks on it and finds yet another client with a similar story deciding to leave their agency.

Without wasting another moment, she rolls away from her desk and storms out of the office. *I've got to talk to Sophia,* she thinks. *I need to tell her about everything I've been thinking. I know she'll listen.*

She practically flings Sophia's office door open and says, "We need to talk."

"Woah." Sophia looks up from her desk with wide eyes. Her blue light glasses glint with the reflection from her overhead light. "What, are you breaking up with me?" she laughs, but Gisela bites her lower lip with worry. She can't bring herself to join in on her friend's humor.

"No," she replies, nearly breathless. "I just need to talk about some things. Can I sit?"

"Of course." Sophia's smile quickly fades into a frown and she gestures to the corner of her office, where two plush velvet armchairs and a wooden bookcase are tucked against the wall.

Her office is very warm and cozy, and decorations cover both her desk and the walls. There are flowers, paintings, posters, and even a few framed pictures. One picture on the desk is of the two of them posing together back in college. The other is of her, her parents, and her younger sister.

Gisela can't help the fondness that wells in her heart as she looks briefly around the room. She loves how different Sophia's work environment is from her own, even though she would go crazy if she had to sit all day in a room so visually stimulating.

She sits down in one chair as Sophia settles into the other. She leans towards Gisela and brushes a lock of dark hair behind her ear, worry evident in her features. "What's up?" she asks.

Just like that, Gisela spills everything to her. She talks about Auri's strange behavior, their kiss, Lucien and his strange interest in both her *and* Monika, and all the odd behavior exhibited by the foreigners.

She even mentions the weird conversations she's overheard between Monika, Jurgen, and the foreigners, even though she wants nothing less than to implicate her childhood friends in something suspicious.

When she is finally done word vomiting, Sophia simply sits back and watches her with a thoughtful expression.

"Well, I won't say I told you so," she teases lightly. They both laugh softly and Gisela presses her head into her hands.

"What do I do?" she asks, voice muffled. "I don't want our business to crash and fail. I love it so much. And I just came up with all these great ideas... what do we do, Soph?"

"Well," Sophia says slowly, "I know you don't want this, but maybe we should consider removing the clients who have been problematic. We can reach out to those who have left, apologize, let them know we are kicking out these clients, and offer discounts or added benefits for them to come back."

"I suppose," Gisela sighs. She slowly sits back up. "That reporter lady is still sniffing around, apparently. I've seen her hanging out in the front a few times, and I've even caught her talking to some of the clients. I'm just worried she's going to get to the ones who are leaving and try to come up with another piece to bash the agency with."

"She might," Sophia says with a shrug. "We just have to keep our heads up and roll with it." When she sees the distraught look in Gisela's eyes, she leans forward and grasps her hands in her own. "Whatever happens, we're in this together. And we're not going down without a fight. This place is too good. We're doing a good thing, Gisela. I promise."

Gisela nods slowly and lets out a long breath. Her friend's words of comfort do help a bit, but she still feels that roiling sense of unease deep in her gut.

"I have noticed something else weird," Sophia adds. "I've seen some of those reviews, and for every negative one... their date, who always happened to be one of the foreigners, gave them a glowing rating. It just doesn't match up. If their encounter was so negative, why the positivity?"

Gisela frowns. "I didn't notice that," she admits, "but that is weird."

"I'm telling you," Sophia huffs. "I've had weird feelings about these people all along."

"I know," Gisela sighs.

Suddenly, the door slams open and Monika's fuming countenance peeks inside. When she notices they are both there, she slides in and closes the door behind her.

"Gisela," she barks. "I will never forgive you for setting me up with that… that dog!"

"What?" Gisela shakes her head. "What are you talking about? Lucien?"

"Yes, Lucien!" she snaps. She sighs deeply before slumping against the door and rolling her eyes. "I'm just being dramatic; it's not really your fault. But that man is absolutely insufferable."

"What did he do?" Gisela questions.

"I…" Monika bites her lip and looks away. Just like their last meeting, it seems as if she's hiding something she doesn't really want to. "He's just a jerk," she mutters. "He never changed, and he's still going down the same road he has been all these years. And he only wanted me for one thing."

"Sex?" Sophia asks, eyes wide.

Monika laughs and shakes her head. "If only it was just that," she murmurs wistfully. "No, it's something I can't even give him." With that, she quickly leaves the room once again, and Gisela and Sophia are left to look at each other in befuddlement.

"That really happened, right?" Sophia kids after a moment. "She was really in here?"

"She was," Gisela answers. "And Sophia… as suspicious as these strangers are, I hate to say there's something not quite right about Monika and Jurgen either."

Sophia's gaze is somber as she meets her eyes. "I was hoping you'd be the first to say it," she admits. "I didn't want to upset you, but I've been getting the same weird feelings from them as I have with the newcomers," she hesitates before adding, "and from Auri too."

Gisela nods and bites her lip hard. "Me too," she whispers, somehow hoping if she says it quietly enough, it won't be heard and, therefore, won't be true.

Chapter 20

Cryptic messages received

When the time comes for Gisela to meet with her Oma again, she doesn't show up. Bast doesn't call. Though she feels a little uncertain and disappointed with the lack of communication between them, she can't bring herself to be around her right now.

She still feels like she is hiding information from her. In fact, it feels as if almost everybody in her life is hiding something, and it doesn't make her keen on trusting any of them.

She feels as if she should be able to trust her Oma, especially since she's her family. She's her only family, and it hurts even deeper to be treated with coldness and insincerity. Still, she tries to keep her head up and keep pushing through the weeks.

Work is a decent distraction, so Gisela finds herself working extended hours at the agency to keep her mind occupied. Auri has been scarce ever since the interview with Roxanne, and there's an unfamiliar ache in her chest every day he doesn't show. It feels as if something is missing, like his presence alone was filling up some hidden part of her she wasn't even aware of.

Even though she doesn't trust him either, she can't help how much she misses him. Mia and Sophia have both told her she should move on, though, and that she deserves a man who will make up his mind about her.

One evening she is working late after Sophia has already left for the night when Lucien, of all people, storms into the building.

As she looks up to see his figure approaching her office, she mutters darkly, "I should've locked the front door."

He bursts into the room, a frenzied look on his face. "Gisela," he spits, "I need your help. I need you to match me."

She looks up at him tiredly; she can't even muster the energy for exasperation anymore. "Come in," she sighs.

His dark eyes widen in surprise before he nods and traipses in slowly. When she gestures to the seat across from her, he quickly sits down.

"Why do you think you should be matched?" she asks. "You're just as impatient, rude, and arrogant as before. I don't think you're ready to have a date. You blew up that date with Monika, and she's not even a client. Leben and Lieben is already at risk right now because of the other foreigners screwing up their dates, and we can't really afford another… high risk."

She doesn't know why she is unloading all of this information on him. His eyes narrow more and more as she goes on, but there is something almost soft about his expression, as if he is actually listening.

"I'm sorry," he mutters. He looks down at his hands. "Can I just look through my potential matches, please? I just… really want to meet someone."

Maybe it's her tiredness or the desire to distract herself with something, but Gisela relents. She shrugs before firing up the matching program and generating a set of matches for Lucien. When the profiles are pulled up, all six, she prints out each woman's page and hands the small stack over to him.

He takes his time with each woman, his gaze scanning over their information and photographs almost hungrily. She watches him scrutinize and debate. He spends at least five minutes or more on each one.

He's definitely a man on a mission; she just wants to know what that mission is.

Finally, he finishes up, neatly stacks them back together, and hands them over to her with a look of defeat scrawled across his chiseled features.

"None of them are… her," he says. "The eyes… they aren't right."

Gisela's mouth twists down and she raises an eyebrow. These cryptic words are practically normal to hear now, but a small part of her rears up in alarm when she hears them.

"The eyes?" she asks.

"Yes," he replies quickly. He looks up at her, and she can't help noticing the unmistakable dilation of his pupils. "None of them have eyes like yours, Gisela."

Her breath catches in her throat, and suddenly all her weariness is gone. The last thing she wants is to be involved with Lucien, especially when she is still pining after Auri. Still, his words scratch at some deeply ingrained itch within her and a suppressed desire to be… desired.

She clears her throat and shifts uncomfortably in her seat. She doesn't want to be flattered, yet color is rising in her cheeks, and her heartbeat is starting to pick up.

"You're beautiful, Gisela," he whispers.

Oh my god. She clenches her hands on her seat and looks away. *What should I say?* A moment passes in loaded tension before she finally mumbles a quick, "Thank you."

"Auri really fumbled the bag with you," Lucien adds.

Gisela's head snaps up and she narrows her eyes. "What?" she asks.

"Well, it's clear you like him," Lucien goes on. A smirk is building on his face as he leans back and crosses his arms behind his head. This gesture alone is enough to snuff out any and all attraction gathering in Gisela's chest. "And it's clear he's turned you down."

She scoffs before looking away and scowling. "If all you're going to do is sit there and ridicule me, you can go ahead and leave," she snaps.

"No, no," he hurries. Suddenly, he is standing up and moving around her desk. He kneels down beside her and grabs her chair to swivel it around so she faces him.

Her eyes go wide as she looks down at this strikingly handsome man, currently kneeling before her with his hands beside her thighs. She swallows the building lump in her throat. She can't deny she's been aching for a sliver of affection and desire, but this is still the last man she wants to achieve it from.

But still… Her mind wanders for just a moment as she glances down at him. She wonders briefly how his lips would feel on hers and how his hands would fit against her waist. *Would it be better than with Auri? Doubtful. But would it be nice?* Color blooms in her cheeks and she quietly chews her bottom lip.

He stares into her eyes and the smirk falls away.

"Gisela…" he murmurs. "Please go on a date with me. Tonight. I want to take you on a picnic and gaze at the stars."

Every logical fiber in her body is screaming at her to remain determined and reject him once again. But something deeper, more primal and perhaps desperate has her murmuring one word: "Yes."

***

Less than half an hour later, Gisela finds herself standing with Lucien in a small local park with not much more than a few benches, a set of swings, a large tree, and a view of the river.

Still, the night air is lovely against her bare arms, and the view of the glistening sky feels more breathtaking than usual.

He has gathered an interesting conglomeration of food items from late-night delis and bakeries, and they both carry a couple of grocery bags as they walk toward a spot underneath the tree.

The air is thick between them, and Gisela's heart is racing constantly in her chest. *I never thought I'd end up here with Lucien. I thought it would be Auri.*

Her heart pangs at the realization, but she swallows down the pain and chooses to flash a warm smile at her date.

He helps her take a seat in the cool grass and she lets out a small gasp as he wraps an arm around her waist and tugs her close.

There is a dull heat between them, amplified by the sudden touch, but it's nothing like the roaring flame she feels when she's with Auri. Still, it feels nice to be wanted and to be begged for.

Should I feel bad for leading him on? she wonders. *It doesn't feel fair to him to be thinking of someone else.*

They begin tucking into their food, and Lucien is surprisingly tender and affectionate in his behavior. She's never seen this side of him, and it feels like it should be endearing, but she can't shake the feeling that something isn't right.

Part of her wonders if this sudden personality shift is even real.

They chat quietly at first, but the conversation is sparse. When they finish their food, though, he turns to face her and pulls one of her hands toward his mouth.

She gapes in surprise as he presses a gentle kiss against her knuckles. Nervous butterflies flutter in her stomach, and he flashes her a dazzling grin.

"Gisela," he says, "I was hoping I could get to know some more about you tonight. I want to know about your childhood and how you grew up."

"Oh," she replies slowly. Not many people have asked her this before, and he catches her off guard with his suddenness. She's started learning to expect surprises from him, though, so she quickly plays along.

She begins by telling him she was raised by her Oma and never knew her parents. She tells him she's lived in Kreuzberg her whole life, met Monika and Jurgen at a young age, and that she's always dreamed of owning her own business.

"Do you, by chance… have any memories from before you lived with your Oma?" he asks, lifting his brows. Like, weird dreams even or anything like that?"

She bites her lip and looks up at the sky. She ponders for a moment, but her memory is mostly blank up until she was around six years old.

"Not really," she admits. "I only really remember stuff from after I turned six. Is that weird?"

He pauses for a moment, then shrugs. Something is dancing in his eyes, though, but she's not sure what. She thinks briefly about trying to use her powers to reach out to him but figures it isn't even worth trying. *Whatever I do, it just doesn't seem to work on their people.*

"I'm not sure," he answers. He inches closer with a smile and reaches out to run a hand through her honey-colored hair. She inhales sharply as his fingers graze her cheek.

She's not sure if she wants him to kiss her or not. When she thinks about the possibility, all she can imagine is the smoky taste of Auri's lips on her own.

He brushes his hand up to the side of her head and presses his palm against it. "Just try to think of something," he whispers, "anything."

She furrows her brow and opens her mouth to protest, but a dull sensation suddenly fills her head.

It feels light, almost as if someone has injected her skull with helium and it is floating up above her. It's not like the sensation of shifting, though, because she is perfectly aware of her body. Pictures and memories begin flashing through her mind, and her body becomes heavy. She can't form a single coherent thought as her mind's eye suddenly becomes like a forgotten album of recollections.

It's almost like somebody is reaching in and shuffling through every single thing she's ever experienced. This is the final conscious thought she has before her brain becomes completely numb.

It's hard to say how long it lasts, but when she rouses, her back is facing Lucien, her head leaning against his chest. It feels as if she's blinked and missed a whole fragment of time.

His hands are on either side of her head, gently running through her hair.

"Are you alright?" he asks. "You seemed like you passed out just then."

She bolts up, her face crimson, and turns to face him. "I—I don't know," she stammers. "I don't know what happened, but…"

A picture suddenly appears in her mind, and her eyes widen. "I remember something," she whispers, "very vaguely, but…"

She tells him about a dreamlike memory she has from when she was three years old of sitting in a grassy clearing beside a pool of swirling, mysterious water. She describes two blurry figures beside her, but she can't place who they are or imagine their faces.

Something seems to click in his mind, and he hangs on to every word with eager anticipation.

When she finishes her story, he sits in silence for at least a minute. "Thank you for sharing," he finally says. He glances down at the watch on his wrist, which is encrusted with tiny color-shifting jewels. "It's getting late, and you seem pretty tired. Maybe we should get you home."

Gisela nods, her mind still fuzzy from whatever happened minutes ago. She lets him help her to her feet and walk her all the way to her house. All of it is a blur as she struggles to sort through her messy thoughts. Finally, they say goodnight and she stumbles all the way up to her room.

Even as she lies in bed, she can't make sense of anything in her brain. Every part of her now feels heavy and dense, and all she can remember before she supposedly passed out is feeling as light as a balloon.

With these brief musings in mind, she drifts into a restless sleep.

Chapter 21

Excuse me!

Throughout the night, Gisela experiences the strangest dreams she ever has. They flit back and forth between scenes; in some, she is standing in that same field she described to Lucien, panicking as the swirling water of the pond rises and morphs into a raging tornado of wind and water.

But when the scene changes, she is floating in a dark void when Auri's voice rings out around her.

She can't make out his words until he calls her name, and she turns all about to try and find him.

But he isn't there.

His voice calls and calls, and she swears she can feel his presence wrap around her like a warm blanket. It comforts her for a moment as she allows herself to sink into the invisible embrace. It always shifts back to that strange, frightening field, though, and the cycle continues until she awakens.

In the morning, she struggles just to get out of bed. Her body feels achy and heavy, and she practically drags herself up and into the shower to get ready. The hot water eases her pain just enough for her to get dressed and shoot a quick text to Sophia, letting her know she'll be late.

When she finally makes it into the office, memories of her date the night before with Lucien come flooding in.

Of course, the fact that he is standing in the middle of the lobby with Auri and two other foreigners doesn't hurt.

As soon as she sees his face, her eyes widen. She glances between him and Auri, and her stomach twists. *Why do I feel guilty? Me and Auri are nothing. He doesn't want anything. So why does the fact I fantasized about Lucien's mouth make me feel so gross?*

She mumbles a quick greeting before walking past them. Sophia is standing in front of her office with a concerned look on her face.

"What's up?" Gisela asks. She stretches her arms above her head and lets out a loud yawn as she approaches.

Sophia turns to her and sighs. "I guess I'll just get to the point," she mutters. "Gisela, did you really sleep with Lucien after work last night?"

Gisela freezes. Her blood runs cold. Her hands begin to shake. "Excuse me?" she barks. "No! Of course not! We—he… took me on a date. We had a late-night picnic, but that's it. Why?" Fear and anger rush into her face as she stumbles over her words, and she watches as Sophia's face contorts with rage.

"That asshole," she mutters. "Gisela, Lucien has been bragging to everyone who would listen about how he finally 'conquered' you last night and got you to sleep with him."

Gisela's jaw drops. She clenches the tumbler in her hands and breathes short bursts through her nose. "That's what I get for giving him a chance," she sneers. Without another thought, she turns and storms back into the front lobby, where Lucien is laughing it up with his buddies.

Auri, however, remains quiet.

His back is as straight as a board, and a quick scan of his posture tells Gisela everything she needs to know about how he's feeling.

His arms are crossed and that normally gentle expression is completely gone. His jaw is set and there's a vein popping out of his neck. His eyes are cold and unfocused, and his brow is rigidly set.

There's no time for her to feel hopeful about his response, though. She whirls on Lucien and, for an instant, wishes she could spit in his face. "Consider yourself removed from the agency," she fumes, lacing all the venom she possibly can into her voice.

Lucien gapes at her, slack-jawed, and lets his arms hang at his side. He quickly gathers his composure and says, "Come on, babe, I didn't mean anything by it. It's just fun. I'm just spicing up the story."

"Well, spice it up with somebody else," she hisses, "because there will be no more stories between you and me. And I want you to leave this building right now and never come back."

"You're overreacting," he argues. His face is twisted into a sneer. "The way you were looking at me last night, I know you would have led me right up to your bed if you hadn't passed out."

At this point, Gisela is seeing red. Before she can say another word, Auri moves in a flash and grips Lucien's collar like a vice. He slings him around in one quick movement and shoves him up against the wall behind them.

"Listen to me, filth." Lucien is squirming under him, but Auri only presses harder against his windpipe. "You're going to take your sorry ass out of here. You are never going to speak to Gisela again. You are never going to look in her direction again. If I find out you have, I will hunt you down and kill you. In fact, you are going to figure out a way to get home as soon as possible. If you're still in Berlin or anywhere on this planet within twenty-four hours, you can count your blessings if I let you live."

Lucien's eyes bore into Auri's with a hatred so intense Gisela can hardly breathe. The air is sucked out of the room around them, and the other two men stumble out of the door.

Sophia runs into the lobby with panic all over her face until she sees Auri and lets out a soft gasp.

"You're lucky I'm letting you walk out of here without my fist marks all over your face," Auri mumbles. "You should know better. What you're seeking isn't good for the Collective." He finally releases Lucien, who hunches over and gasps for air.

As soon as he recollects himself, he stands up and dusts off his suit. "Fine," he snaps. "I'm leaving. I'm leaving this hellhole for good. I didn't find what I was looking for anyway." With that, he storms out of the building, leaving the three of them to stand there in utter silence.

Gisels doesn't understand the last words Auri spoke to him or what Lucien declared right afterward, but she feels as if it carries some meaning weightier than she could ever imagine.

"I'm sorry you had to see that," Auri whispers. When she looks up at this fierce, powerful, protective man who looms above them like a solid tower, all she can see in his eyes are doubt and defeat.

"Thank you for standing up for me," she breathes.

"And thanks for getting rid of that jerk," Sophia quickly adds.

"You didn't need me," Auri laughs. He turns to face Gisela and his face softens. "You were amazing by yourself. I just couldn't…" he groans, "I couldn't take the way he was talking to you." His bright eyes lock on hers and she feels her breath hitch in her throat in a delightfully familiar way.

Something passes between them silently, and even with all the questions and frustrations building in her mind, Gisela feels her heart melt with each passing second. Sophia must sense something is happening because she ducks out of the room without another word.

Not a moment after, Auri strides confidently across the room and sweeps her into his arms.

Her face is pressed to his chest, and she can feel his heart beating just as wildly as hers. For a bittersweet, lovely moment, it feels as if they are one, and she wishes they could stay like this forever.

He pulls away and presses his hands to her cheeks. "Gisela, my Liebling," he murmurs, "you are a precious pearl in a sea of empty oysters. Please, never change."

His words set her whole body aflame, and she can barely muster a breath as she whispers back, "Never."

Then his lips crash against hers, but this time they are slow and insistent. Time slows down and completely consumes them as they fold into each other, and she finds herself panting and weak in his arms. Her knees buckle and she gasps as he moves his mouth slowly down her neck, spreading a wildfire everywhere he touches.

"Auri," she gasps. He presses her back to the wall behind her and returns to her mouth for one final kiss.

It doesn't last long enough, though, and soon he is pulling away.

He stares down at her, and it almost seems like there are tears building in his eyes. "I know you have questions," he blurts. "I'm sorry, Liebling. I can't answer them. It isn't time."

"What do you mean it isn't time?" she demands. "Why do you have to hide yourself from me? Why is everyone hiding themselves from me? I trust you. I just need to know what's going on." The desperation builds in her voice until she is on the verge of tears herself, but he simply pinches his own eyes closed and shakes his head.

"I'm sorry," he replies. And just like that, he removes his hands from her waist, and she feels empty without his touch. Then he is gone, and all that is left is the tinkling sound of the bell above the door and her swollen, grieving heart.

Chapter 22

Need for friendship

After everything blows up, Auri disappears once again. This time, though, it somehow feels more final. Gisela can hardly bring herself to work, but she knows it's the only thing that can take him off her mind. She notices that most of the foreigners gradually drop out of the agency, but she can't bring herself to care.

So for the next few weeks, she busies herself with planning events, sorting through sign-up sheets for lessons, and coordinating all of her fun, new plans for Leben and Lieben.

Her heart isn't fully in it, though, and all of her friends can tell.

One evening, as she is finishing her nightly unwinding routine and slipping into a cozy matching sweat set, her doorbell rings. Oliver lets out a high-pitched meow and scurries down the stairs ahead of her.

Curious, she heads downstairs and peers through her peephole, only to find all six of her friends huddled at her doorstep. Sophia is holding two bottles of wine, Klaus is carrying a pack of hard cider, and Jurgen is holding a few pizza boxes.

She furrows her brow, unlocks the door, and opens it. "Guys?" she asks. "We didn't plan anything, did we?" She looks them up and down and notices they are all in lounge clothing, just like her.

Sophia laughs. "No, silly." They all shuffle in, and she continues, "We just thought you seemed like you needed some cheering up." She edges closer and her eyes flash with sympathy. "And maybe some advice," she whispers.

Gisela smiles softly and nods. "Thank you," she says with a gulp.

She welcomes them in and grabs some cups and plates from the kitchen as they start setting everything up in her dining room.

"We can eat in the living room," she announces. She watches a few of them share amused glances; she never lets anyone eat in the living room except for herself. But she doesn't feel like doing anything other than curling up on the couch and watching reality shows. "Just please… don't get anything on the white sofa."

Mia giggles and Klaus looks at her with a warm smile. Monika laughs and Jurgen gives an approving nod.

No matter how odd this little group of people is, especially when it's composed of both childhood friends and college ones, she appreciates it more than she could ever vocalize.

They all gather up their pizza and alcohol and head to the living room, where Sophia has already started up recorded episodes of Gisela's favorite show. They all talk and laugh as they watch ten different men all vying for the same woman's hand in an over-dramatic, most likely scripted reality competition.

Eventually, though, Gisela feels all her pent-up feelings and anxieties just aching to explode out of her. She is sitting between Mia and Sophia, clutching a pillow in her arms as she rests her head on Mia's shoulder and talks.

As she begins to spew out everything that has happened between her and Auri, they all listen with mixed reactions.

Mostly everyone watches with expressions of sympathy or protectiveness, but Monika and Jurgen look somewhat uncomfortable. She talks about his strange words, choosing to leave out the fact that she's heard Monika and Jurgen say similar things themselves. Part of her wonders if they will reveal anything tonight when given the opportunity.

As she passes over that part of the story, they both visibly tense up, but neither says a word.

When she finally finishes with the most recent encounter, the room is silent for a whole minute.

"I... don't know what to make of this guy," Sophia admits. "One minute, he's looking and acting totally weird and suspicious, and the next, he's defending you from creepy assholes. I don't know whether to hate him or love him. But one thing's for sure. He shouldn't keep treating you like this."

"I agree," Mia adds. She shifts in her seat as everyone's attention turns to her.

Jurgen, in particular, watches with keen interest.

"I mean... he's pushing you away and pulling you back. It's playing with your emotions. You don't deserve that."

"It's frustrating, to say the least," Gisela mumbles. Her face is growing beet red the longer they talk about it and the more she thinks about their stolen kisses. She subconsciously presses her fingers to her mouth.

"In all my time of knowing you," Klaus begins slowly. "I've never seen you so worked up, distracted, and distraught. It worries me, Gisela." She smiles up at him as he gazes down with an empathetic gaze. Oliver is currently curled up in his lap, purring loudly; she isn't surprised her cat has taken to Klaus so easily.

Sophia is sitting next to him, and Gisela doesn't fail to notice his hand reach out and twine with hers. She watches the heat bloom in her friend's cheeks, and her mouth twitches up in a smirk.

Klaus is the definition of warmth and reliability, and she's so glad her best friend has him in her life now.

"I don't know," Monika says from the other side of the room. All heads snap in her direction. "I mean, it sounds really upsetting. But I kind of understand why he's acting this way."

"You do?" Gisela asks. Her breath catches in her throat, and for a moment, she's hopeful that Monika is finally going to spill the beans.

Jurgen cuts in, though, and says, "I think Monika is just saying that he seems conflicted. He does like you, but for some reason, he isn't ready to be in a relationship, or maybe he just can't because he has other commitments back home."

Monika looks down at her wine glass, avoiding eye contact at all costs.

Gisela bites her lip. "Maybe…" she murmurs.

"That doesn't make his behavior right, though," Sophia quips. "He's a grown man. He can control himself. It doesn't give him the right to put her feelings through the wringer."

"Sure," Jurgen replies. "You're right. We're just saying… maybe this is why he's been doing it."

The group falls silent again. Hans, like usual, makes no move to contribute to the conversation. He sits beside Monika, slowly sipping at his cider. When Gisela looks at him, though, his eyes are full of distress.

Maybe Monika isn't the only one itching to give away some secrets, she muses.

They continue watching the show, and the conversation gradually turns to new subjects.

At the end of the episode, though, Sophia stands from her seat and pulls Gisela up with her. They rush to an empty bathroom and Sophia closes the door behind them.

"What is it?" Gisela asks, but she has a feeling she already knows.

"I think those suspicions we talked about the other day… they're right. Did you hear the way Monika and Jurgen were talking?"

Gisela nods. "I'm sure they're hiding something."

"We need to really investigate now," Sophia says with a deep breath. "Something sinister is happening, and we need to find out what. Are you ready to do some digging?"

Chapter 23

"Touche"

Gisela's friends end up crashing at her house that night since they stay up late talking and drinking. She has a few guest rooms, and as she stays up with Sophia watching TV, she watches with curiosity as each person retreats to a room.

Mia and Jurgen both leave within a few minutes of each other, and Gisela shares a knowing look with Sophia. Next up are Monika and Hans. Finally, she feels like a third wheel sitting in her own living room. She can feel the tension coming off of Sophia and Klaus in waves.

There is probably one last guest room, and she doesn't need to stick around to know who's going to occupy it.

She loudly says goodnight before heading upstairs to her own bedroom. As soon as she hits the bed, thoughts of Sophia's recent words to her fill her mind.

"How exactly am I going to dig?" she asks herself. She screws her eyes shut in frustration, trying to think of something she can do, but she is too tired.

Part of her wants to resign and give up on ever finding anything out. As she starts drifting off to sleep, though, she realizes she never could. If she doesn't discover the secrets her friends are trying so hard to bury, she fears it's going to eat at her until she all but disappears.

***

Throughout the next week, Gisela and Sophia return to work as usual. They have plenty to organize and carry out around the agency without piling on investigative work, but in every free moment, they can find they are planning.

It's good for Gisela; it takes her mind almost completely off of Auri.

They talk about potential suspects they can confront and search for answers. Jurgen is clearly more resolute than Monika, but even Monika doesn't seem eager to let anything slip. Plus, their familial bond is more likely to keep her mouth shut.

As they are sitting and plotting in Sophia's office one morning, Gisela suddenly asks, "What about Hans?"

"Hans?" Sophia's eyes go wide. "He works with Jurgen. Why didn't I ever think about that?"

"He was being a little shifty that night at my house," Gisela continues. "He looked really nervous, actually. I'm almost certain he knows *something*. And you remember how secretive he and Jurgen were at their building. Maybe it's time I pay him a visit."

Sophia nods excitedly. "I agree. You should text him and ask to meet up. He may be more guarded if you just show up at their door. Besides, Jurgen will be there, and I'm sure Hans won't say anything when he's around."

Gisela sighs. "You're right. I just hope he'll say anything. even without him around. I can tell something is happening between him and Monika, and I'm sure he wouldn't want to betray her either."

"You're right," Sophia concedes. "But we can still try."

Gisela whips out her cell phone at that moment, and they lean closer together in the space between Sophia's two velvet armchairs. She holds her phone out so Sophia can watch as she drafts a text to Hans.

> Gisela: Hey Hans. I know this is out of the blue, but I was wondering if we could meet up and talk sometime. I have some questions, and I'm hoping you can answer some of them. Let me know ASAP.

Sophia nods in approval and Gisela hits send.

They wait with bated breath for a minute; Gisela is about to stand up and walk away, thinking he probably won't respond yet anyway, when her phone chimes with a notification.

She hastily opens her phone and they both skim the screen hungrily for his reply.

Hans: Sure. Not at the company or the agency, though. Let's get lunch. Tomorrow at noon?

Gisela looks up at Sophia, who is wearing a nervous grin. She decides to push her luck.

Gisela: Today at noon?

The bubble pops up at the bottom of the screen, letting her know he is typing. It stops for a moment as if he is contemplating on the other side. Then, a final text comes in.

Hans: Okay. See you at noon. Let's go to Redding's Diner.

As Gisela tucks her phone back in her pocket and exchanges a look with Sophia, she realizes this is the moment everything becomes serious. This is the moment that will change everything, and as she examines the uncertain look in her friend's eyes, she knows both of them are thinking one thing.

This is either going to result in nothing or set off a nuclear explosion in their entire friend group.

***

When Gisela arrives at the diner for lunch, Hans is already waiting at an outdoor table. There is a pinched expression on his face. His forehead is creased as he looks into the distance, his stubble has grown out more than usual, and his dark hair is a little longer than he normally lets it grow, sweeping about an inch lower on his forehead.

"Hans," Gisela greets, pulling her chair out and sitting down slowly. "How are you?"

Hans turns to her with a tired look in his eyes. It seems as if he's been fighting some internal battle, and as soon as she notices it, she realizes any revelations she's going to make will not be anti-climactic.

"I'm fine," he grunts. He takes a long sip of his drink and sighs. "I've already ordered for us. I think I got your usual right."

Gisela gives him a gentle smile. The two of them used to eat here sometimes when the rest of their friends were too busy and they wanted somebody to bounce ideas off of or receive sound advice from. They've always been the most serious members of the group, and Gisela has always appreciated his stern nature.

He keeps the group grounded in his faithfully stoic way.

She's hoping today she can appeal to that side of him, who she knows is still faithful to his friends, even if he is tangled tightly in whatever web Jurgen, Monika, and Auri have bound him in.

They don't make much conversation as the server brings their food and they dig in. They're both stewing in their own thoughts, and each one of them knows what this meeting is truly about.

Finally, Hans decides to break the silence. "I know why you're here," he announces. "Gisela, I'm sorry, but... there's not much I can tell you."

Gisela furrows her brow and stares at him. "I don't know if I believe that," she responds. "I think you just don't *want* to tell me. Actually, I think you *do* want to, but you feel like you can't."

Hans tenses. "How can you see right through everyone?" he mumbles. He pushes around his food for a second, staring with narrowed eyes at his plate.

Gisela laughs. "Sometimes I wish I didn't," she admits sadly. "Sometimes I wish I could be as trusting or as carefree as Mia or as openhearted as Klaus. But as we both know, we can't change who we are."

Hans nods. "I know," he murmurs. He drops his fork and looks up at her. "Listen, Gisela. I've signed some... binding... contracts. I can't go into detail, but it's way more than just a legal matter. There's a lot at stake. I won't sugarcoat it. My *life* is at stake."

Gisela sucks in a breath of air and waits in silence. Her stomach is turning violently and she feels as if she may throw up.

"So I *can't* tell you much of anything. I'll say one thing, though. Auri, Monika, and Jurgen are not who they seem. They aren't even… *what* they seem."

Gisela feels as if the world is spinning around her. *What could that possibly mean?* She wonders. *They're not what they seem? Why the emphasis on that word?*

"Do you understand me, Gisela?" Hans' voice grows more urgent. "You need to be careful around them. I know you've known Monika and Jurgen your whole life, but you can't trust them. You can't trust them or the foreigners. Any of them. They're all the same. Do you get it, Gisela?"

She's trying to make sense of his words, but her whole head feels as if it's tilted on an axis, and everything she thought she could always be sure of has been flipped upside down. She forces herself to hone back in on his words. She nods. "Yes, I think so."

"Good," he replies slowly. His gaze lingers on her before he looks into the distance. "Keep looking," he urges, "but do it carefully. I don't even know what they're capable of. I only know a sliver of what they're planning because that's all I've been told." He looks at her, and she gulps.

He lowers his voice to a whisper and starts to fish something out of his pants pocket. "Reach under the table."

She blinks in confusion but obliges. She connects her hand with his and feels him press something small, cold, and hard into her palm. *A key.*

"That's a key to exactly where you think," he mutters. "They keep odd hours. I suggest if anyone were thinking of paying a visit, uninterrupted, arriving between the hours of three and five in the morning."

Gisela nods. The lump in her throat is keeping her from getting out any words. Her adrenaline has spiked to an all-time high, and she knows she won't be able to delay this mission any longer than possible.

Finally, she manages to get out two small words, "Thank you." He nods and gives her a terse smile, but fear is already creeping into those cloudy, green eyes.

***

When Gisela returns to the agency, she doesn't feel lighter or relieved like she had hoped. Instead, a heavy cloud has descended over her, and her mind is even more fuddled and confused. She spends a few minutes alone in her office, just processing before she tells Sophia what Hans said.

"Do you want me to go with you?" Sophia asks her.

Gisela shakes her head. "I don't want to put you at risk," she says. "I don't know what the hell is going on, but Hans made it sound like there's danger waiting behind those doors." Her mind flits back to that mysterious door Hans refused to let them see behind. "I'm just going to sneak in, try to find something, and sneak out."

"Are you going to be okay going out that late? Or, I should say, early?" Sophia kids, but she can't hide the weariness from her tone. Without saying it, they both recognize this situation has become far more serious than they anticipated.

"Yeah, I will," Gisela assures her. "I doubt I'd be able to sleep anyway."

They spend the rest of their work day in tense trepidation, neither of them able to get much done, but not wanting to go home because their minds will only torment them more fiercely. Sophia decides to spend the night at Gisela's, so they can at least keep each other company while they wait for 3:00 a.m. to roll around.

They spend the evening and night watching more reality TV and eating leftover pizza, but even the cringeworthy drama unfolding before them isn't enough to distract their minds. They mostly sit in silence as they watch, both too distracted to laugh and too nauseous to talk about what's on their minds.

Finally, the time comes, and Sophia sends Gisela off with a wordless hug. She squeezes her tightly, expressing all the care and appreciation words cannot convey in one simple embrace.

Gisela looks back at her with a nervous smile and teary eyes before getting in the cab she called and riding over to the building of Hans on Tech.

She has the key Hans gave her in her pocket, and when she's dropped off, she scurries over to the front door. She's never unlocked something so quickly in her life, and as soon as she slides inside, the automatic lights in the front lobby click on.

The room is just as barren as it was on her first visit with Sophia, but there is a familiar bag sitting on a small coffee table against the wall. Her breath catches in her throat. *Is Auri here right now? Hans told me nobody was here at this time.* The adrenaline is pumping like liquid courage through her veins, and now the only thought she has is to look in that bag and get out as soon as possible.

She darts over to the table, her steps light, and yanks it open. There isn't anything particularly interesting in the main compartment, but there is a zip-up pocket against the side that seems to call her name.

Carefully, she slides open the zipper and peers inside. Something is glimmering within, and when she reaches in to pull it out, she feels cool metal against her fingers. Slowly, she draws out a long golden chain. It looks jarringly similar to the bracelet Auri wears, with a million colors dancing off of every link when it shifts in the light. However, at the center of the chain, there is a round, dime-sized pendant.

Really, it's a gemstone. It's not like anything she's ever seen. It has a dull sheen across its surface and is a dark mossy green that reflects like an oil spill when she shifts it in her palm.

Just as she's fully admiring this beautiful jewel, quick footsteps sound from down the hallway.

He's here. She quickly shoves the necklace into her pockets, not sure why she's even drawn to it, and shuts Auri's bag. She steps back towards the door, hoping she can make it outside before he finds her, but it's too late.

He enters the small room just as she places her hand on the door handle, and the air around them sinks like fog.

"Gisela," he greets, voice cool and level. She can't figure out what the look is in his eyes, but his stiff posture and composed voice let her know that one, he's been expecting her, and two, he isn't pleased. "What exactly do you think you're doing?" he asks, taking a step in her direction. "You aren't supposed to be here. And how did you get a key?" His eyes dart to her hand, which is still clutching the small silver key. She grips it tighter, her knuckle growing white.

"None of your business," she snaps. "Why are you here? This isn't your building."

His eyes flash with amusement. "Touche," he replies. "However, I happen to have express permission from the owners. Can you say the same? Oh, and I mean both of them."

He is clearly bothered, but there is no anger or malice in his voice, which only confuses her more. *When will I know where his allegiance lies? Does he even have any?*

Suddenly, all the memories of the moments they've shared and the unspoken feelings between them rise up her throat like bile. Tears well up in the corners of her eyes and she takes in a shaky breath. There's no more stopping this up; it's time to let it out.

"You've been stringing me along for too long," she shouts. "Auri, I think I'm in love with you, you stupid jerk." His silver eyes widen at her statement, but he doesn't seem that surprised. "When are you just going to give it up and admit you love me too?"

She puffs her chest up as a wave of boldness floods through her. "You try to stay away, but no man who doesn't care for someone the way you do for me would go to such lengths to protect me and look out for me. No man who doesn't love someone kisses a woman like you've kissed me." Her voice grows louder. "No man who doesn't love someone looks at her the way you look at me!" She is screaming now, her voice echoing around the small room so intensely it feels like they are trapped in her own head.

"Just admit it," she cries out, the tears finally bursting forth and rolling down her cheeks. "Just say you love me!" She lets out a loud sob and crumples to the floor, no longer holding any authority over her own emotions or even her body. She's never felt anything this acutely, and it alarms her how much it rattles her to the core.

She can't see his face because her vision is too blurry from the tears, but his silence is palpable. Finally, he takes a few long strides toward her and kneels down.

He tilts her chin up with a finger and delicately wipes away most of her tears. A small flicker of warmth lights up her belly, and just when she thinks he's going to sweep her into his arms like he's done before, he utters the coldest words she's ever heard him speak.

"Gisela, Liebling, I don't love you. I will never love you. I've been stringing you along this whole time for my own amusement." He pauses for a second, and his words snuff out all the building heat inside of her like icicles smothering a flame. "You mean nothing to me."

He pulls away his hand and stands back up before turning around and retreating back down the long, dark hallway he came from.

Gisela sits for a moment, stunned. The automatic light shuts off and she is left there in the dark. She allows herself to stay put for just a minute, silently hoping he will come back and tell her it was all a cruel joke, before gathering herself up and picking up her phone to call a cab.

She shuts off all the feelings waging war in her mind so she can get herself out the door and home safely. Only once she's home and slumping into Sophia's waiting arms does she allow herself to break.

Chapter 24

Riddence and boundaries

After that night and her fated confrontation with Auri, Gisela feels as if everything within her is broken in two. Sophia stays by her side into the morning and holds her on the couch as she cries and cries for what feels like hours.

When she is finally done crying and the sun is beginning to rise, Sophia puts on her comfort movie, wraps her in a blanket, brings her water and a snack, and brushes her hair as she eats.

It feels as if the tears never really stop, even after they've calmed down. She constantly has liquid seeping from the corners of her eyes until they are so red and aggravated from rubbing at them that she has to hold warm rags against them for a shred of relief.

She and Sophia both fall asleep on the couch at some point, and she is more thankful than ever that they can set their own hours and open their building whenever they please. When they wake up sometime in the afternoon, Sophia decides to head in and make sure everything is running smoothly. She tucks Gisela back in after forcing more water down her throat and reassures her she will be just fine at work without her.

At some point, Gisela manages to get herself in the shower and freshen up, but she crawls into her bed immediately after. Sophia returns that night and sits with her when she wakes up, already prepared with ice cream, water, and more movies.

As potent as the heartache is within her, Gisela reflects once again on how kind and steadfast Sophia's friendship is.

Days go by, and Gisela decides to take a week off from work. The agency is mostly self-sufficient anyway, but Sophia can handle any problems that may arise.

She spends her time moping in bed, sitting up, watching movies with Sophia and Mia, laying out in the sun in her backyard whenever Sophia urges her to, and sleeping. Something about the whole process feels mildly therapeutic, despite the scolding voice in her head telling her she's being ridiculous and lazy.

She's thankful she has Sophia and Mia there to remind her that voice is wrong and that it's good to take care of herself. She's also endlessly thankful for her cat, Oliver, a sweet and constant companion through each dreary day.

The one thing she doesn't do at all during the entire week is practice her powers. She hasn't felt the desire to do so in almost a month now, and a part of her wishes she could just give them up completely.

She also finds out from Mia that Jurgen has been acting rather odd around her. His initial attraction to her has turned into an almost obsessive fascination with her life and her career. He is constantly asking about her job writing articles and broadcasting news.

Gisela doesn't voice it to Mia because she is unsure if she should burden her with these worries, but she wonders if it is all a part of whatever scheme Jurgen and Monika have been plotting.

Still, Gisela dreads the day she will inevitably have to return to work because there will be reminders of Auri everywhere she looks. Also, the mystery surrounding him and the foreigners still needs to be solved, and she won't be content until it is.

Near the end of the week, she is doing some stretching outside in the late afternoon sunshine with Sophia. She is finally starting to feel a little more like herself, but the words that come out of her friend's mouth nearly send her toppling over.

"Hey, Gisela," she says slowly. It's clear she is anxious about something even before she says it. "I just wanted to let you know that Auri has been lurking around the agency lately. There are still some of the foreigners in our system, so I've let him come in to help out with them, but he's been grumbling about missing some kind of necklace or something. And," She hesitates, "he's been asking about you."

This is exactly when Gisela stumbles, but she barely manages to keep her balance before transitioning out of her position and standing upright before fixing Sophia with a horrified stare.

"You couldn't have told me sooner?" she asks, feeling more resigned than actually upset with her.

"I didn't want to throw your progress off track," Sophia explains. "I didn't want him to be on your mind more than he already was."

Gisela lets out a long sigh and plops herself down on her yoga mat. "That's fair," she concedes. "I appreciate you, Soph."

"You're welcome," she replies with a sly smirk. She follows suit and sits down cross-legged across from her. "I wanted to ask… do you know about that necklace he's been looking for? You didn't take something when you went there, did you?"

It dawns on Gisela at this moment that she never explained to Sophia the amulet she pocketed. "Actually, I did," she admits, nervously biting on her lip. "Come inside. I'll show you."

She leads Sophia into the house and up to her office. She's stowed the necklace inside a drawer in her desk, underneath a discreet false bottom. She's never had a use for it before, but she's glad it's there now. She pulls out the shimmering gold chain and lays it on the desk for Sophia to examine.

They both admire the exquisite piece for a few minutes, turning and twisting it in the light to observe all of its intricacies.

"I've seen this type of jewelry on the other foreigners," Sophia notes. "Monika and Jurgen too. What do you think it means?"

Gisela shrugs. "Honestly, I'm not sure it means anything. It could just be something linked to their culture, but…" she pauses and takes in a deep breath. "This sounds crazy, but it doesn't look like anything from this *planet*."

"Girl, we've been through plenty of crazy," Sophia laughs, "at this point, aliens could come down on earth, and I wouldn't be surprised."

Gisela lets out a snort. "Yeah, right," she teases, "aliens, sure." She rolls her eyes. They both giggle for a few moments before returning their attention to the strange necklace. "I did feel some kind of pull toward this," Gisela admits, "like I couldn't keep my hands off of it. I just feel like it's something significant, and I'm hoping we'll find out."

"Hopefully sooner rather than later," Sophia notes solemnly, "before Auri burns the whole agency down trying to find it."

A chill rolls down Gisela's spine at the thought, and she suddenly realizes she has no idea exactly what he is capable of.

***

When the weekend comes, Gisela is finally ready to go back to work. She feels antsy, knowing there are still answers to uncover and work to throw herself into at the agency. Still, having a couple of more days to rest and ponder her next move will prove useful.

She spends most of her time writing out notes and typing up more plans for Leben and Lieben on her home computer. She is able to access their program from home as well, so she even manages to check in on some clients and send out new matches.

Of course, she feels a pang of hurt each time she does. It feels like a brutal reminder that her one potential "match" has slipped away. Rather, he shoved her off of him and bolted.

Still, she pushes through, knowing it will be even harder going into L and L and confronting all of it head-on. The thought that she will also have to confront Auri lingers in the back of her mind, but that is the one thing she refuses to touch mentally.

Sunday morning, as she sits with a cup of iced coffee at her desk, feeling like the embodiment of comfort. She has her feet propped up in the chair with her and she is clothed in comfortable fuzzy lounge pants and a soft sweater. It's the day before she returns to work, and she finally feels level-headed.

Then, her phone rings, and the name of her Oma flashes across the screen. She draws in a deep breath, remembering today will mark the second meeting with her she's missed. Slowly, she reaches out and answers, putting the call immediately on voicemail.

"Gisela?" Bast's voice rings out, clear as day, into the room. "Where are you? This is the second meeting you've missed."

Hearing her talk reminds Gisela of all the coldness she's shown her in recent months. It also reminds her of all the secrecy and refusal to tell her the simplest things, like what her mother was like when she was still here.

Bitterness fills her throat like foul medicine, and she scrunches up her face.

"Hello?" Bast shouts, reminding Gisela she hasn't said anything.

"I'm sorry, Oma," Gisela replies, a surge of courage flowing through her. "I won't be meeting with you anymore, at least for a while. Not until I know I can trust you, and not until you trust me enough to tell me about my mother. Call me again when you're ready to do so. Goodbye, Oma." Before Bast can get a word in edgewise, Gisela hangs up.

A rush of sadness hits her like a cresting wave, but with it comes a quieter reassurance that she has done the right thing. *Mia and Sophia are right. I need to learn how to take care of myself. If that means setting boundaries with my own Oma, so be it.*

***

Gisela returns to work the next day, feeling both confident and unsettled. She knows what is waiting for her behind that door, and even with the knowledge of who is waiting there, she knows it will still be just as hard.

She walks inside the building and is immediately greeted by the sight of Sophia and Auri standing in the lobby.

Tension is obvious as her friend glares daggers in his direction and folds her arms tightly against her chest. It's clear she's been standing here waiting for Gisela to arrive so he can't ambush her by himself.

"Gisela," he says as soon as the door closes behind her. He rushes toward her. "I need to ask you something. I'm missing a necklace. It has a small, round amulet on it. The chain is gold. It's very important to me. Have you seen it?"

His tone is frenzied in a way she's never seen from him. His complexion is pale and there are bags beneath his eyes. For a brief, flickering moment, she imagines he's been missing her just as much as she's missed him, but it quickly gives way to the truth of the matter.

He hasn't spent any sleepless nights thinking about me—just his stupid amulet.

She brushes past him without a word. Now that she is here, in his presence again, she doesn't find it as difficult as she had thought. She simply chooses to give him the cold shoulder, even as he follows her frantically towards her office, pestering her along the way about the amulet.

"Please," he begs. "Gisela, if you took it, it's okay. I won't be upset. Just please return it. You don't understand its value."

Her hand is on her door now, but something about his words makes something in her snap.

"No," she seethes, whirling around to face him, "you understand *nothing*, Auri. You don't understand the value of *anything*. You're nothing but a greedy coward who's hiding something very dark and very sinister. And you can bet whatever you'd like that I'm going to find out what."

With that, she steps into her office and slams the door behind her. Despite the feeling of power she gains from telling him off, it takes every bit of willpower not to succumb to tears once again. She hears some harsh, muffled words exchanged between him and Sophia on the other side of the glass and turns to watch him storm out of the building completely.

Good riddance, she thinks. But she doesn't really mean it.

Chapter 25

"Enough"

Gisela and Sophia find themselves at a loss for what to do next when it comes to their investigation. There's nothing more Hans can tell them, and Monika and Jurgen have both made themselves as scarce as Auri has ever since their last confrontation.

It feels strange, this distance between Gisela and her childhood friends, but she doesn't know what she would do if she were to talk to them. She worries she might snap and confront them, demanding information, and this would likely be way too drastic for her own good.

Hans' words still echo in her mind on a daily basis, reminding her there is more at stake now than she can truly understand. Knowing that she needs to protect not only herself, but the rest of her friends as well, is enough to keep her writhing hunger for information at bay.

So they throw themselves into their work with fervor. They begin hosting speed dating sessions at the agency twice a month, as well as cocktail and dance nights every other week. Their schedules are kept stuffed to the brim, but the agency has been booming more than ever.

She has documents upon documents filled with even more ideas, just waiting to be unleashed as well. She wants to host game nights, movie nights, and, eventually, annual themed parties for her clients held in Berlin's biggest ballroom.

But she's trying not to get too far ahead of herself.

Working hard on this agency is about more than just working for her, though. It's about creating and fostering a thriving community that's welcoming to all and helps people make meaningful, potentially lifelong, connections.

Perhaps the biggest idea she's been nesting is the plan to eventually launch a brand new feature of the program meant to pair up friendship matches as an alternative option to romantic ones. She wants everyone to have a friend group as close and comfortable as her own, even if it's currently in shambles.

Divided loyalties will do that.

Just when everything is starting to look up for Leben and Lieben, a report with the potential to shatter their entire livelihood is published in the paper, and there is no amount of online posting they can do to stop the explosion of chatter and conversation surrounding their blossoming agency.

Gisela sits with Sophia in her office on the same day the article is published, only hours later. They've done everything they can on social media, with Mia's help, to prepare for the ensuing onslaught of criticism, but nothing can truly prepare them for the storm of scandal brewing in the distance.

Rain is pounding against the windows as they sit on the floor between the velvet chairs, legs stretched out on the small area rug. They are stunned silent as they read an article detailing every single suspicious behavior their foreign clients ever exhibited.

It reads like a tell-all exposé, and Gisela can't help but feel flummoxed, wondering why this writer has been so hell-bent on destroying their careers. There are even quotes from former clients who had left the agency due to their horrible dates, describing the oddness of the men's behavior.

The writer talks about people seeming to vanish into thin air, wearing strange otherworldly jewelry at all times, treating their matches with utter disregard as soon as they realized they weren't interested, and "laughing in the face of Kreuzberg and all her people hold dear."

Gisela scoffs at the dramatic proclamations splattered all over the page, but she knows this is exactly the kind of writing readers will eat up.

When she reaches the end of the article, the pen name waiting at the bottom comes as no surprise. *Roxanne Philpot.* Rage stirs like a caged animal deep in Gisela's gut, but right now, there is nothing to do about this and nowhere to unleash it. She feels completely and utterly helpless.

"I don't know what to do," she mutters to Sophia. "Who knows what this will do to our image?"

Sophia slumps into her. "I don't know either," she admits, "maybe we can release some kind of public statement? We can post it online and maybe even get in touch with the clients who came back after they left. We can prove we've taken action to make sure our clients are safe and valued. We have to."

Gisela takes in a shaky breath and squeezes Sophia's hand. "I used to be the one who grounded your anxiety," she jokes. "What happened?"

"Tables have turned," she kids back. She gives her a squeeze in return, and this simple moment is comforting in and of itself. "That's what best friends are for. It's a give-and-take. And I know one day I'll be the one breaking down and needing your wise direction."

Gisela smiles and closes her eyes. "We'll get through this," she whispers. It's a promise, not just to Sophia, but to herself.

A loud bang resounds through the building as somebody bursts through the front door. They look at each other and bolt to their feet before exiting the office and hurrying down the hallway.

Monika and Jurgen rush into the main room right outside of Gisela's office, their eyes wild and filled with a thousand unnamed emotions. Primarily, Gisela can make out fear. She can only think of one thing that could possibly ignite this dramatic reaction in them, and yet it doesn't quite make enough sense.

"Monika? Jurgen?" she asks, crossing her arms.

The tall brunette woman brushes her hands over her tailored pants and lets out a series of long, shaky breaths. It sounds as if she sprinted all the way here.

"Have you two seen the article?" Sophia asks.

Monika's eyes narrow and her nostrils flare, but before she can respond, Jurgen steps forward.

"You could say that," he snaps. "How could you two allow this? This woman is jeopardizing this entire operation! All your clients are going to start dropping like flies!"

"Operation?" Gisela asks, contempt dripping from her voice. Suddenly, all of her pent-up outrage comes bubbling to the surface, and she clenches her fists at her sides. "Are you kidding me? What are you talking about, operation? This isn't an operation; this is our business and our livelihood. If anybody knows the stakes here, it's us. And why the two of *you* are having such an intense reaction to this, god only knows. But I am about tired of your crap."

Monika's eyes widen and her entire demeanor deflates. "Gisela," she says, reaching out to her friend.

"No." Gisela steps back. Her voice has lowered, but her fiery rage is replaced by icy cool. "I know you're hiding something. I don't know why, but the two of you are unusually invested in my business. I should have guessed there was something up from the start with how enthusiastic you've been to help us." She shrugs. "I guess I trusted you. I just assumed you were our friends."

"Gisela, please," Monika pleads. She steps towards her and latches onto her arm. "You can trust me! I am your friend. Just listen; we need to tell you something."

Gisela has never seen her friend this desperate, and for a moment, she considers dropping her guard one more time.

"We aren't telling them anything," Jurgen fumes. His face is set in stubbornness, and he is staring pointedly at his sister. "It isn't the time."

"If not now, when?" Monika screeches. "I'm so tired of this act, Jurgen!"

Gisela rips herself away from Monika. "Enough!" she shouts, her voice silencing the room immediately. "I don't want to hear it." She turns her piercing gaze to each sibling, one by one. "I don't know who you two are anymore."

A gasping sob escapes from Monika's mouth before she quickly covers it with her hand. Gisela ignores the tears freely streaming down her face. She's never seen her cry before in her life, but at this point, she doesn't know whether to believe they're even real.

"I'm going to find out what's going on for myself," she mutters darkly. As soon as she starts walking towards the door, Jurgen steps into her path. Something dark and serious swirls in those eyes, and for a moment, fear grips her body. *Would he actually harm me?*

Then she remembers those strange and unexplainable powers buried within her, the same ones she's tossed to the wayside for the last two months. She thinks back to Auri when he commanded the reporter to leave in such a way that seemed to force her compliance and wonders if that same kind of power is resting in her.

She concentrates all of her focus and energy on the hulking man in front of her, but instead of seeking out his mind to connect, she seeks out his very willpower.

Gisela sucks in a long, deep breath, feeling it fill every fiber of her being, and pushes her own iron-like will into every word she utters. "Jurgen, stay out. Of. My. Way."

For a moment, she worries it hasn't worked. Jurgen appears to wrestle with her will as it shoots out of her like a spear and latches onto his own. It's like a mental brawl as they stare into each other's eyes.

And then, as if a cloud has rested on top of him, his entire body relaxes. His expression loosens into one of dull submission, and he steps out of her way.

She doesn't know how long this hold on him is going to last, but she isn't going to stick around to find out. "Sophia!" she calls out, but her friend is already hot on her heels. They race out of the building and spot a taxi dropping someone else off half a block away. "I'm going to head to the tech building," Gisela pants as they race down the street.

Thankfully, they make it just in time to climb in. "You go wait at my house. You know the code to get in." Sophia stares at her with wide eyes but simply nods. It's obvious Gisela is on a mission.

She pauses to give the cab driver directions, and then they're off. She can feel the weight of Auri's amulet keenly in her jean pocket, and for the first time, she knows what she needs to do with it.

She doesn't know why; all she knows is that as soon as she finds Auri, she needs to put that necklace around her neck and find out what he's really been hiding all this time.

***

When they reach the building of Hans on Tech, Sophia pulls her into a reassuring hug before sending her on her way.

She strides towards the door with nothing but the anger-fueled determination to keep her going and hastily unlocks it with Hans' key. As the door clicks open, she practically thrusts herself inside. There is no sign of anyone in this room, and when she pauses for a moment to listen, no footsteps come down the hall.

She sets off down the sterile hallway, knowing exactly where she needs to go. At this point, she is thankful for her photographic memory and incredible propensity for directions. She follows the same winding path that Hans took her and Sophia on their first day here.

It only takes a few minutes for her to reach the same four-way intersection they stopped at before. This time, she gazes towards the heavy golden curtain with its mysterious designs and smirks, knowing nobody is here to stop her from going in.

She slows down as she steps toward it and traces her fingers over the material. Something pulls at her gut in the same way she felt pulled towards Auri's amulet. She doesn't know why, but something inside of her is calling to whatever's inside this bizarre and foreign curtain.

With that final thought, she forcefully pushes through the part down the middle and steps into a huge warehouse of a room, all open space and high ceilings.

It isn't the magnitude of the room that catches her eye or the fact that Auri is standing in the middle of it.

No. What draws her attention is the ten-foot-tall golden portal at the back of the room, alive and humming with energy as blue, green, and purple matter swirls like a vortex at its center.

"Oh my god," she breathes. Her head suddenly feels light, and she stumbles forward. Her heart is pounding like a drum in her ears, and everything inside of her is screaming at her to run with all her might straight into that portal. It's like a carnal instinct that pushes aside all other thoughts or logical reasonings.

She forgets all about Auri, Monika, and Jurgen or what they've been hiding from her. She even forgets the necklace that only moments ago felt so heavy in her pocket. All she can hear in her mind is a screaming, echoing cadence of, *Home! Home! Home!*

She takes another step forward, preparing herself to run, when Auri turns toward her with eyes as wide as saucers. Time stills completely, and even as he opens his mouth and yells something at her, all she can hear is her own mind yelling at her to go, go, go.

He starts to run toward her, and she can feel her limbs weakening. Her head is dizzy and she can see darkness beginning to close in on her vision, but she can't bring herself to stop until she reaches that portal.

Just as she's slamming right into Auri's firm figure, and his arms loop under her arms to catch her collapsing body, she watches as one of her former clients steps right out of the portal and into the room.

At that moment, all goes black.

Chapter 26

Damn! didn't see that coming

Gisela slowly blinks into awakeness, and as soon as she does, the bellowing sound of the portal behind her startles her into alertness. Auri's arms are the only things holding her up as she is half-sprawled on the floor.

She looks towards the portal, and that same carnal desire to launch herself inside it begins to stir once more. However, the other foreigner steps across some thick wires running from the machine to the wall and leans over to pull a switch hidden from sight.

In an instant, those swirling colors collapse inward and the portal is empty. The revving noises have stopped and the room is utterly silent.

Gisela stirs in Auri's arms and he helps her to slowly sit upright. She stares at him, blue eyes full of alarm, stricken and speechless.

He gives her a gentle smile before brushing his hand across her cheek. "Gisela, my Liebling," he murmurs affectionately. For a moment, she leans into his welcome touch, and warmth seeps throughout her entire body. She closes her eyes with a deep sigh.

Why does it feel like ages since I've felt his touch?

Just like that, the moment is fractured, and everything he's done to her comes flooding back in a cacophony of painful memories. She yanks her face away, ignoring the distraught expression on his face, and scoots a few feet away from him.

"You..." she mutters. She opens and closes her mouth several times. Her brain is so scrambled; it's as if someone's cracked it open and cooked it like an egg. She can't organize her disorderly thoughts or begin to string together any kind of coherent sentence. She chooses instead to narrow her eyes at him and soak in the dismayed look on his face.

"Gisela, please," he begs, "come here. Let me help you."

"Help me?" she cries out. A loud, unhinged string of laughter escapes from her mouth and she throws her head back in hysteria. When she finally calms down, she looks back at him and frowns. "You can't help me. You don't love me."

As she speaks those words aloud, it feels as if she is taking his blade and stabbing it into her own heart for him. To her, it's at least better than letting him do it himself.

His eyes begin to well with tears. "Gisela, Liebling, I…" He stops and trails off before tearing his eye contact away.

As her memories of the day begin rushing back, Gisela reaches for the necklace in her back pocket. *It's still there.* She pulls it out in one swift movement and watches as Auri's eyes turn frantic.

"What are you doing with that?" he asks, voice shaking. "Gisela, give that to me."

Without saying a word, she drags the chain over her head and settles it against her neck. As soon as the amulet presses against her flesh, the world around her shifts.

"Oh my god," she whispers.

The man standing in front of her is not one she recognizes in the slightest, at least at first. Once she gives her eyes time to adjust, she slowly realizes his features are still the same. Those silver-blue eyes are the same piercing hue, and his hair is just a tinge lighter.

Aside from these grounding details, nothing else is right. His skin is a pale blue color, and there are strange antennae-like appendages protruding from the top of his head. "What the hell…" her voice trails off and she turns to look at the other man in the room.

He is blue as well, and his white hair is cropped short against his head. He has the same pale eyes and the same thin stalks sticking out just above his ears. He is staring straight at her with his lips pressed tightly together. She can't remember his name right now, but she doesn't care.

"This is what I was afraid of," Auri whispers. Gisela stares at him, trying to process the words coming out of his mouth even as her mind wrestles with the sights before her.

"This is some kind of trick," she stammers. "You did something to this amulet to make it—to make me—" she halts in her words and gasps for air. With trembling arms and legs, she scrambles to her feet. Auri stands as well, gazing at her with nothing but sadness.

She knows, deep down, that this is no trick. This is the secret. This is what they've all been hiding from her. *At this point, I won't be surprised if Oma was in on some of this too.*

"But…why?" she asks, her throat tightening and drying up. "What is this? What are you?"

Auri sighs and takes a tentative step towards her. He halts for a second when she flinches, but when she doesn't move away, he rushes in to press his hands against her waist.

The touch is achingly familiar and warm, just like the Auri she's been getting to know all this time. Just like *her* Auri.

She gulps and tries to muster a smile, but she feels so weak and confused.

"This is why I've kept myself from you as best as I could," Auri breathes. "I don't know if you'll believe me, but I am from another planet called Atlantida. We came here to…" He trails off before letting out a deep breath.

"We can get to that part later. Gisela, Liebling, I am so sorry I hurt you. It felt like the only way to protect you from the truth. It wasn't your time yet. But Gisela, please know…" He pauses, and those silvery eyes soften with something she's never seen in them before. "I'm very much in love with you."

His voice, deep and rumbling like a purr, makes her knees buckle and knock together with those words. He catches her and holds her up until she can steady herself.

"How do I know you're not lying to me?" she asks, her voice as small as she feels.

"I promise," he urges, "I love you, Gisela. I truly do."

"But?"

"But I cannot be with you." The sadness returns to his gaze. "I wish I could fully explain why, but that knowledge isn't really mine to give. It just isn't time for me yet. And there are countless mysteries and responsibilities awaiting you in the future. I don't know if I'm worthy of being a part of it all."

She furrows her brow at him. *Once again, he is talking in riddles when all I want is for him to speak plainly and honestly. Is that really so much to ask?*

She pries herself away from his grip and immediately feels her body ache for his touch. *I have to stay strong,* she wills herself. As she stares into Auri's eyes, she wants with all of her might to believe everything he's saying.

However, that lingering bit of doubt races back and forth, replaying every horrible, careless word he spoke to her.

Truthfully, she feels entirely torn between believing in him and fearing what he's capable of.

"Please, Liebling," he pleads, "trust me."

She starts to open her mouth, her answer waiting cautiously on the tip of her tongue.

Then she rips the necklace off of her body, breaking its chain in the process, and throws it to the floor.

Epilogue

Bast is sitting in her home on the river when she feels a sharp pang of distress echo throughout her body. She winces.

Gisela is in trouble, she realizes. She's always been able to feel her pain as if it were her own, which is why her relationship with Auri has been tormenting her so much. She's tried to warn her away from him, but somehow she is just too stubborn to listen.

I know where that comes from, she muses. *I still wish she would just listen. She's finding out too much. It isn't her time yet, and she isn't ready.*

She sighs and sets down her mug of hot tea on the counter. "I need to talk to you," she whispers. The image of her partner's handsome face rises to her mind, and she smiles fondly. Gisela looks so much like him.

She sets herself down right there on the floor and breathes in deeply. In just a moment, she feels her essence separate partially from her body, so she splits her consciousness between her non-corporeal being and her physical one.

She watches from above for a moment as her physical body stands and continues to go about her daily tasks. She breathes deeply once more and careens herself down miles of endless astral wavelengths with the force of a stampeding wildebeest.

Beautiful colors and shapes flash and gyrate around her for just a few seconds, and then she is there on her home planet. Atlantida.

She morphs herself into a resemblance of her physical body and drifts down to the floor of her kitchen. All is still and quiet inside the house; she smiles when she realizes her children are away at their learning synagogues. Her heart pangs through the pride she feels, and she wishes she could see them again, even for a moment.

Just then, her partner, Rael, appears from around a corner. His golden-hued hair hangs in a thick curtain of waves around his shoulders. The sight of him walking unknowingly toward her has her heart lodged in her throat.

He looks up and his pale eyes immediately alight. "Bast, my love!" he exclaims. He rushes towards her and pulls her into his strong arms. She runs her own hands up his chest, relishing in the warm firmness of his muscles beneath his shirt. This is a man who's spent his whole life laboring to create a beautiful home for them. He is strong in many more ways than just one.

She smiles into his lips as he envelops her in a smothering kiss. Every time she sees him, his eagerness never wavers. It makes her feel like they're newlyweds all over again, first signing their contract and declaring their vows to one another.

All the stress of her life on Earth melts away as she gives herself to his touch. He kisses his way across her jaw in playful pecks, and she laughs in delight. Finally, he pulls away and gazes at her with the warmth of a thousand suns in those bright, yellow eyes.

"Oh, how I've missed you," he declares, pressing his face into her neck.

"I was just here a few days ago," she teases, but she understands completely. Each day they are apart feels like a lifetime.

They spend a few more minutes relishing each other's company before she pulls him away to the balcony. They stand together, hand in hand, and look out across the rolling blue hills of their beloved home. A home that has been crying out and dying for years now. A home that needs the life force of its people to keep going and providing. And their people have been slowly dwindling for decades now; they truly need a renewal as soon as possible.

"I have much to tell you," she says with a deep sigh. She leans into his strong, comforting presence. "Gisela has wrapped herself up in too many complicated matters. I fear she may find out the truth sooner than we anticipated."

He tenses for a second before breathing deeply in. "If she finds out about our planet sooner than we thought, maybe our timeline just isn't exact. She will be thirty soon, remember."

"Not for another year," Bast quips. "I'm sorry, I'm just frightened."

"I know you are," he croons. He pulls her closer, wrapping an arm around her waist. "We can't protect her fully forever. At some point, she has to come into her own."

Bast nods. "Yes, you are right."

They stand together in silence for a few more minutes as the blazing red sun rises over the horizon.

"I think the Restless ones in the east are starting to make plans," he murmurs. "I've heard talk recently that they're searching for the Oracle."

"Yes," Bast confirms, her lips tightening into a straight line. "One from their colony actually came to earth, seeking her out there. I only hope he doesn't find what he's looking for."

"I hope for all of our society's sake, he hasn't and never will," Rael adds. "We already have enough to watch out for, let alone a group of violent rebels vying for control."

Bast laughs dryly. "Oh, honey, just you wait. I have a feeling the days about to come are only going to grow more complicated, more tense, and more violent than ever."

"You're so reassuring," he teases.

"You love me for it," she grumbles with a smile.

Reddish light bathes the blue land before them, turning everything that familiar purple hue of morning.

She realizes there is irony buried in the fact that, as she speaks of the struggles barreling toward them like a bullet, the very land they're fighting to save is welcoming her home with bright, cheerful arms and a burgeoning dawn.

9 781764 238007